Mark re
starving

All other thoughts left his head in a rush. He kissed her eagerly, wanting to taste all of her— her shoulders, the hollow behind her elbow, the slight indentations of her ribs.

She was breathing in sharp pants, her short fingernails clawing delicately against his back, stroking him to incoherence.

Mark leaned down, taking off her panties. He gently felt that she was already damp and waiting for him. He kissed her hips, then her legs, before stroking a quick lick at the juncture of her inner thighs. His erection throbbed painfully.

Sophie let out a moaning sob, her legs finally relaxing and opening for him. She was insanely responsive. And her sounds of desire were driving Mark straight to the edge....

MW00490700

Blaze™

Dear Reader,

Every year I go to a conference for writing, and it's always in a different hotel. I see a lot of familiar faces, since we're all in the same industry, but I also see a lot of strangers, especially in the airport. And one year I got to thinking—what would it be like if one of my heroines met her hero because they were both stranded at the airport? And what if they turned out to be competitors?

Just like that, *One Night Standards* was born.

I hope you have fun reading about Sophie and Mark, and their battle between doing what their minds tell them and doing what their hearts know is right, even if it seems crazy.

Enjoy,

Cathy Yardley

ONE NIGHT STANDARDS
Cathy Yardley

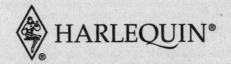

TORONTO • NEW YORK • LONDON
AMSTERDAM • PARIS • SYDNEY • HAMBURG
STOCKHOLM • ATHENS • TOKYO • MILAN • MADRID
PRAGUE • WARSAW • BUDAPEST • AUCKLAND

If you purchased this book without a cover you should be aware that this book is stolen property. It was reported as "unsold and destroyed" to the publisher, and neither the author nor the publisher has received any payment for this "stripped book."

ISBN-13: 978-0-373-79336-5
ISBN-10:   0-373-79336-7

ONE NIGHT STANDARDS

Copyright © 2007 by Cathy Yardley.

All rights reserved. Except for use in any review, the reproduction or utilization of this work in whole or in part in any form by any electronic, mechanical or other means, now known or hereafter invented, including xerography, photocopying and recording, or in any information storage or retrieval system, is forbidden without the written permission of the publisher, Harlequin Enterprises Limited, 225 Duncan Mill Road, Don Mills, Ontario, Canada M3B 3K9.

This is a work of fiction. Names, characters, places and incidents are either the product of the author's imagination or are used fictitiously, and any resemblance to actual persons, living or dead, business establishments, events or locales is entirely coincidental.

This edition published by arrangement with Harlequin Books S.A.

® and TM are trademarks of the publisher. Trademarks indicated with ® are registered in the United States Patent and Trademark Office, the Canadian Trade Marks Office and in other countries.

www.eHarlequin.com

Printed in U.S.A.

ABOUT THE AUTHOR

Cathy Yardley needs to get out more. When not writing, she is probably either cruising the Internet or watching movies. Her family is considering performing an intervention for her addiction to pop culture. She lives in California. Please visit her at www.cathyyardley.com.

Books by Cathy Yardley

HARLEQUIN BLAZE

14—THE DRIVEN SNOWE
59—GUILTY PLEASURES
89—WORKING IT
300—JACK & JILTED

HARLEQUIN SIGNATURE SPOTLIGHT

SURF GIRL SCHOOL

Don't miss any of our special offers. Write to us at the following address for information on our newest releases.

Harlequin Reader Service
U.S.: 3010 Walden Ave., P.O. Box 1325, Buffalo, NY 14269
Canadian: P.O. Box 609, Fort Erie, Ont. L2A 5X3

To my husband, Joe, for giving me my son.

1

IN THE CROWDED AIRPORT car-rental area, Sophie Jones did the only thing she could think of to get out of the jam she was in.

"I have to get to San Antonio!" she yelled.

"Miss, could you please get down from the counter?"

Sophie Jones ignored the car-rental clerk's plea, holding up a sign that said SAN ANTONIO and shouting as best she could over the din of disgruntled passengers. "I know somebody out there is headed to San Antonio. I'll pay for gas. I'll pay the rental fee. But I *have* to get to San Antonio by tomorrow morning. Anyone? Anyone?"

"I can't let you stand up here!" The clerk tugged at the hem of Sophie's skirt.

Sophie scanned the crowd. They were split into two groups: those who had gotten keys to the last of the rental vehicles, and those who, like her, were stranded here in Oklahoma, thanks to the airplane radar error that had grounded all flights in the Southwest. She noticed other people starting to write their own signs, and yelling for their own rides.

The clerk gave a more insistent tug. "I'll call security if I have to."

Sophie sighed, clambering down from the counter. "You have to have rented a car to somebody going to San Antonio," Sophie said, putting on a smile and trying to take the desperate tone out of her voice. "Couldn't you just point out the person going there, so I can plead my case?"

The clerk, a harried-looking woman in her forties, frowned. "I've rented out more cars this afternoon than I have in two months," she said. "You can't expect me to remember something like that."

But there was something in the woman's voice, and her expression, that suggested that she *did* remember. Sophie felt a little surge of hope. "I'm in a terrible jam here, you have no idea. It would mean a lot to me," Sophie wheedled, now increasing the desperation, hoping to play on the woman's sense of decency. And it wasn't as if she were lying. She had possibly the most important meeting of her career, maybe of her life, the next morning in San Antonio.

Beg, borrow or steal, she was getting a ride to San Antonio no matter what.

The woman's eyes narrowed. Then she quickly looked over her shoulders. "It means a lot to you, huh?" Her voice was low, and Sophie had to strain to hear her. "How much is 'a lot'?"

Sophie paused, taken aback. Then she reached into her purse, pulling out a fifty-dollar bill and putting it on the counter.

The woman quickly took the money, tucking it away in a pocket. "See that tall guy, standing in line to get his car?"

Sophie looked over at the chaotic group of people waiting for the few remaining rentals. "Which one?"

The woman smiled. "The gorgeous one. You can't miss him."

Sophie suddenly realized who the woman was talking about. Easily six foot two, with slightly wavy blond hair, he had the kind of masculine beauty that reminded her of Johnny Depp or Brad Pitt. "Holy cow," Sophie whispered.

"He's going to San Antonio," the clerk said, with a little smile. "Him, I wouldn't forget."

"I can see why," Sophie agreed. "Okay. Thanks."

"Don't mention it," the clerk said, and Sophie knew it wasn't a mere pleasantry—the woman didn't want anyone to know she'd been bribed.

Sophie nodded, then took a deep breath. Gathering her luggage and presentation material, she awkwardly made her way to where the gorgeous guy was waiting patiently in line.

"I understand you're going to San Antonio," she said, without preamble. "I need to get there. I was hoping you'd be kind enough to let me share a ride with you."

The man's blue-gray eyes widened in surprise. "How did you know where I was going?" His voice had a Southern drawl, sweet and smooth, like aural caramel.

"Does it matter?" Sophie evaded. "That's where you're headed, right?"

He looked flustered. "Well, yes."

"Then what difference does it make if you bring one more person with you?" Sophie asked reasonably, smiling with encouragement.

"Ordinarily, I'd love to help out," he said. "But I'm getting crammed into a compact car as it is, and I've got a lot of luggage. And I'll be honest with you. I'm coming off of a six-city sales trip, and I'm really in no mood for company."

Sophie gritted her teeth. She'd been traveling a lot, too, trying to get her family's fledgling company off the ground. It wasn't as if she were looking for a new best friend. In fact, the last thing she wanted was to make small talk with a stranger while driving six to ten hours. She kept the pleasant smile fixed on her face.

"I can tell you're a gentleman," she countered, deciding to play on his Southern background. "You'd never leave a lady stranded."

He sighed with irritation. "Like I said, ordinarily—"

"I promise, I won't make a sound. You won't even know I'm there," she said, feeling a wave of despair that she fought to ignore. "It's incredibly important to me."

"I'm sure there are other people headed to San Antonio, who would love to help you out," he said gently. "I'm truly sorry. Really."

Sophie felt tears sting her eyes.

"Listen, can I tell you a story?" She dragged the luggage, keeping pace with him as the line inched forward. "A few years ago, my mother got fired from her job at a cosmetics company. It wasn't personal, just business, they said. I was working at a big firm at the time, and I was sick of seeing things that were done in the name of big business. My mother and sister decided to start their own little cosmetics company, and I quit my job to join them. It's been one of the most important decisions of my life."

He smiled, the act making him look even more hand-some, if possible. "That sounds nice," he said. "Still, I don't see…"

"There's a trade show in San Antonio," she said. "We're showing there."

"I'm sure missing one day won't mean that much," he said.

"You don't understand," she spat, frustrated. "I've got a huge meeting tomorrow morning. It could mean the difference between success and bankruptcy. I *have* to get to San Antonio."

He stared at her, and she held the handle of her roller bag in a death grip. "Lots of people are stuck here," he pointed out. "The radar blackout has been on the news. I'm sure whoever you're meeting with will understand and reschedule."

Sophie laughed. "Unfortunately, I get the feeling that this is my one and only chance. You don't know the person I'm meeting with."

He got up to the front of the line, and took his keys. "If they're that unreasonable," he said, jingling the keys, "maybe you shouldn't be doing business with them at all."

Sophie bit her lip. She'd thought the same thing, since the whole point in starting the company was to get away from that kind of corporate cutthroat attitude. Still, their little brand was floundering, and this would be a huge boost.

"They're one of the biggest retailers in the country," she said. "High end... I'm sure this doesn't mean anything to you, but it's an unbelievable opportunity. Mrs. Marion doesn't wait for anybody. If I don't get there, she's going to think we're not serious." She put a hand on his sleeve. "I'll pay for the rental. I'll pay you for the ride. I'll even do all the driving. But please, *please*...let me share your car."

He studied her face for a long moment, and she held her breath.

"Shoot. I'm not made out of stone," he drawled, and she felt relief flood through her system. Impulsively, she hugged him.

"Thank you, thank you, thank you," she breathed, dancing despite her exhaustion. "You are a saint. You're an angel."

"My mama would've kicked my butt if she found out I'd left a woman stuck somewhere, anyway," he said, and Sophie laughed. "So, this Mrs. Marion is going to be impressed that you did whatever it took to make your meeting, huh? She sounds sort of..." He paused, as if searching for a word. "High maintenance," he finished.

Sophie laughed again as they headed for the car. It was tiny, as he'd said. She felt bad for him, having to accordion his tall frame into the small automobile for the next six hours. "She's that," Sophie agreed. "But she knows that a deal with Marion & Co. is huge, and the fact that she's considering us… I can't even tell you how unbelievable the opportunity is. I really appreciate this."

"You can put your stuff in the trunk," he said. "I have to go get the rest of my bags and things."

"Oh, wait," she said, stopping him before he turned away. "What's your name? I don't even know who I should be thanking."

"Mark," he said, holding out a hand and smiling that mind-blowing smile. "Mark McMann."

She smiled in return. His hand felt warm and firm, and for a second, she forgot all about the trip, and the meeting, and basked in the glow of his attention. "I'm Sophie," she said. "Sophie Jones."

He winked at her. "Be right back."

Sophie quickly packed her luggage and materials into the small compartment, feeling a little guilty at how much room it took up. She'd make it up to Mark, she told herself. The guy was being so nice. Maybe she'd take him out to dinner, thank him properly.

Going out to dinner with a guy that good-looking would hardly be a hardship, she thought with a smile.

Mark returned after a few minutes. "I'll try to wedge most of my stuff in the back," he said, rolling a small dolly's worth of boxes and luggage up to the car.

"Good grief," Sophie said. No wonder he didn't want company. They were going to be crammed like sardines in the tiny car. It was going to be an uncomfortable ride. "Is there anything I can do to help?"

"Again, I wouldn't want to make a lady do my heavy lifting, either," he said, with a quicksilver grin. "This'll only take a minute."

"I don't mind…"

Sophie's voice trailed off as she saw the logo on the boxes. It was distinctive, a set of three *T*s in a swirling script.

Trimera. She'd know that logo anywhere.

He saw where she was looking, but didn't say anything. He simply packed the rest of the boxes in the car.

He works for Trimera, she realized, the relief ebbing away slowly. Trimera, one of the biggest cosmetics companies in the business. The same company, in fact, that had fired her mother.

No wonder he's going to San Antonio. He's going to the same trade show. And he's pretending not to realize we're competitors!

"Okay, all set," he said, in that same pleasant voice. "Shall we?"

She nodded, getting in the car.

And of course, he decided to give me a ride…after I told him about the Marion & Co. meeting.

He got in the driver's seat, smiling at her. "Well, we might as well get to know each other. It'll be a long trip."

She nodded, smiling back at him even though the last thing she wanted to do was smile.

"Why don't you tell me about this company of yours?" he asked, his voice elaborately casual. He didn't even look at her when he asked, simply concentrated on the road as if his life depended on it. "It sounds great."

Had she called him an angel? The guy was a devil— a handsome, smooth-talking, sneaky devil.

And for the next six hours, she was stuck with him.

THEY'D BEEN IN THE CAR for an hour, and the highway stretched out in the distance with very few cars besides their own. The sun was setting in a beautiful wash of salmon, rose and orange out on the horizon.

"That's gorgeous," Mark said, nodding at the sunset.

"Mmm."

Mark bit back on a sigh of irritation. He hadn't wanted to travel with anyone—it was bad enough that he had to drive, instead of catching a few hours of sleep on the plane—but he was being nice enough to offer the woman a ride to San Antonio. And now, since they'd gotten on the road, she'd barely spoken two words to him, and most of his questions had been answered with those one-syllable nonwords. She was so tense, he could practically feel it bouncing around in the interior of the ridiculously compact space they were sharing, threatening to explode. It was like traveling in a grenade.

"Warm enough?" he asked, pointing to the car's climate control panel.

"Mmm," she responded. "Thanks."

He had to get her to open up. Otherwise… Well, not

only would the trip be unpleasantly uncomfortable, but the whole point to them sharing a car would be ruined.

She said she had a meeting with Marion & Co. An important meeting.

He might not be credited with having a lot of business savvy by his colleagues, but he'd worked on the Marion & Co. account and knew them well. It was one of the biggest accounts Trimera had. If they were talking to other cosmetics companies, it would be worth a lot to know what they were talking about.

I find out what's going on, and I might finally get that promotion.

Mark smiled to himself. He'd been working in sales at Trimera for the past five years, patiently biding his time, putting up with the snickers and snide comments about his past. He'd put in his time at night school, getting his MBA. Now, he was looking for his big break to make it up to the next level: director for a big account. He'd been angling for Marion & Co. for over a year. To have Sophie Jones and her information fall into his lap was an incredible stroke of luck.

He glanced over. Sophie's toffee-colored curls danced around her shoulders, emphasizing the curve of her high cheekbones. Her green eyes scanned the scenery, fringed by long lashes. Her full lips pouted ever so slightly.

Having a woman like this fall into my lap would be incredible luck, no matter what the reason.

His body tightened in response. "Great sunset," he croaked.

She glanced at him, her expression slightly amused. "You said that already."

He frowned. "Oh. Right."

He was attracted to her. That wasn't all that odd, but the strength of his reaction was. He was used to dealing with women on a daily basis in his line of work—cosmetics execs were usually female. And before that, doing runway work, he'd been surrounded by beautiful women constantly. Comparatively speaking, Sophie wasn't stunning, like the models and actresses he'd seen. But there was something about her, a spark or something, that he found absolutely irresistible.

"So, you work with your mother and your sister, you said?"

"Mmm."

"That must be fun," Mark continued relentlessly. "I couldn't work with my sister. Or my brother, now that I think of it." He laughed. "And I wouldn't want to work with my mother. Too much pressure. If giving her my grades was hard enough, I can't imagine what it'd be like to give her a sales performance report."

He was gratified when she chuckled a little at that one. "Older or younger? Your brother and sister," she asked.

It was an opening, so he took it. "My sister, Dana, is younger by three years. My brother Jeff is older by two."

"You sound close," she noted.

"Well, you must be close to your family, if you're working with them," he said. "How do you manage without going crazy?"

She smiled. "We do go crazy. Mom's a bit of an absentminded professor," she said, and her expression was soft, unguarded. "Lydia's a creative type. She's younger by only about ten months…a total 'oops' baby. She acts like she's older, though."

Mark nodded, encouraging. "And you're not the creative type?".

"I'm the business type," she said. "Numbers, strategy, you name it. That's what I—" She stopped short, as if she realized that they were, indeed, having a conversation about her company. "I must be boring you, with all this talk," she demurred.

He gritted his teeth. He'd need to try another tack.

She shifted in her seat to face him. "Listen, can I be blunt?"

"Please," he replied easily, shifting gears. Whatever it took to keep her talking.

"I know who you work for. It's right there on your product boxes." She crossed her arms. "You're my competition. You know that."

Now he did sigh. He doubted she would have missed that, but he didn't know that she'd put together that they were competitors. "Well, yeah. But that doesn't mean we can't, you know, talk."

"Actually," she pointed out, "it does. At least, it means I can't talk to you, about business."

"It's not like we're even in the same league," he replied. "No offense intended."

"None taken," she said, her words edged in ice.

"I mean, Trimera is huge. Global. From the sounds of it, your company… What's the name of it, anyway?"

"Diva Nation."

Good name, he thought absently. "It's a small start-up. You're too small for us to be worried about."

"Really?" she said sweetly. "And I suppose mentioning the Marion & Co. meeting did nothing to cause you concern."

She had him there.

"You can't honestly tell me that you're asking about my company out of the kindness of your heart," she added. "I mean, you seem nice enough, but you've been trying to pump me for information since you got on the road. Don't kid a kidder. I used to work for a big company, too. Nothing's too small to be a threat. You're looking for an angle." Her voice was bitter. "I remember what it's like."

He realized she was right—and her comment made him feel ever so slightly slimy. "It was just business," he said, knowing it was a lame defense.

She shook her head, her curls twitching in response. "It always is," she murmured.

"How old are you?" he asked.

She blinked in surprise. "Twenty-nine," she responded. "Not that it's any of your business."

"I just thought—you're awfully young to be that jaded."

She sighed. "You're right. But I've had some bad experiences."

"Why don't you tell me about them?"

"What are you, a bartender?"

He chuckled. "You don't have to tell me about your business now, if you think it'll compromise you," he said. "But you could tell me about your old job, right?"

Glancing over, he saw she was staring at him through narrowed eyes. "Are you trying to soften me up?"

"Yeah," he admitted, and was rewarded when she laughed. "But I am interested."

"Know thy enemy, huh?"

"We've got another five hours ahead of us, at least," he said. "I don't want to be stuck feeling like a spy or a criminal just because we happen to work in the same industry." He winked at her. "Besides…I like you."

That seemed to catch her by surprise. "Why?"

"You've got guts," he said. "And lord, you're persistent. I half thought you were going to hit me on the head and steal my car if I didn't give in!"

"Why didn't I think of that?" She laughed again, and slowly, he felt the tension in the car recede. "So, what do you want to know?"

He looked at her. "Why don't you tell me about your old job," he said, "and we'll take it from there."

Sophie revealed her past as an account executive at a cutthroat apparel company, talking about hellish bosses and asinine corporate policies that had finally caused her to quit. The stories, while crazy, were also funny, at least the way she told them. "So that's why I decided to work for my family," she said. "What about you? What caused you to work for cosmetics?"

"I used to be—don't laugh," he cautioned. "I was a male model."

She didn't laugh. "I can see that," she said instead, and he could've sworn that there was a tone of admiration in her voice. Warmth expanded from the pit of his stomach in response, and he focused on her next question to distract himself. "But why cosmetics?"

"I ran into a lot of cosmetics people working," he said. "They knew a lot of cosmetics sales reps, and I wound up interviewing with one of them when I decided to go into business. It was a friend of a friend. Besides, I understood how the products worked on the women I worked with," he added. But that sounded defensive. "I figure, it's been a good experience."

"Huh. We're a pair, aren't we?" She leaned back, stretching, and he got a glimpse of her breasts pressing against the straining cloth of her blouse.

"How do you mean?"

"We've both got something to prove," she said. "I'm trying to prove that you can make it in business without being heartless. You're trying to prove that you're more than just a pretty face."

He stared at the road, momentarily stunned. She'd summed up his life in one sentence, and realized what people he'd been working with for years hadn't seemed to grasp.

"I'm sorry," she said quickly. "That was blunt, again, wasn't it?"

"No, it's fine," he said.

"I know you're more than just your looks, though," she added.

"Really?" He sneaked a quick look at her face. "How can you tell?"

"You heard me talk about my meeting, and you jumped on it," she said. "You've been persuasive, without being a pest. And you listened to my old business stories and asked really good questions. You obviously know your stuff."

He couldn't help it. He grinned with pride. "Thanks."

"You're going to be a tough competitor to beat."

He laughed. "Damn, I like you."

She smiled in response. "I like you, too."

"Let's stop talking about business," he said. "I want to know more about you. The real you."

She laughed, a bit nervously. "What do you want to know?"

"Anything," he said softly. "Everything."

For a moment, it was as if they were frozen in time. Then she cleared her throat.

"I always wanted to live in Paris."

He smiled. It might not help him get the promotion, but as he listened to her talk about her dreams and fears, he admitted that he felt better than he ever had, at any sales meeting or business function. And she was, technically, the enemy. After this car ride, they'd probably never see each other again, except the odd mention in a trade bulletin.

Too bad she's a competitor, he thought, putting his

ambition aside for a moment as he listened to her musical voice.

Because I sure would like to get closer to this woman.

"WE'RE FINALLY HERE," Mark said, his voice sounding slightly disappointed.

Sophie could hardly believe it. It was eleven o'clock when they rolled into the Bedingfield Arms, and yet the hours had flown by. Considering they'd both avoided talking business, she was surprised at how much they did have to talk about. But he'd traveled around the world, to many of the same cities she'd loved. And they liked a lot of the same movies, the same books, the same music. And while she was exhausted, she was sorry that the trip had to end.

"Oh, man, I am dying for a hot shower and a big bed," he said, in that mint-julep drawl of his.

She sighed. That sounded good. Sounded even better if she could share one or both with Mark, who was arguably one of the best-looking men she'd ever seen. And the past few hours had only made her bizarre crush stronger, because he was different. Good-looking guys with egos the size of a Cadillac, she wanted nothing to do with. But Mark was funny, and versatile, and smart. He knew how to listen, and he knew how to share…. He had some of the wildest stories she'd ever heard. She'd actually wiped tears away from the laughter several of his anecdotes had produced.

If only he could write a decent e-mail and knew how

to return a phone call, she'd probably go to bed with him, she thought, then bit her own tongue as she started giggling.

"What? What'd I miss?"

"Nothing," she said, rolling her own head back, trying to stretch the kinks out of her neck. "Just punchy."

"You are the best, you know that?" he said as they parked the car. "Honestly. I haven't had this much fun on a road trip since the Parker twins needed a ride to Georgia."

"Well, I'd love to drink to the Parker twins, and you'll have to tell me that story sometime," she said, unfolding herself from the car with a groan. "But looks like our sojourn is over, pal."

They collected the bags, and she felt a stab of regret. Now that they were at the hotel, he'd undoubtedly go up to his room, she to hers, and never the twain would meet, as it were.

Still, he was funny, he was nice, and she hadn't spent this much time with a man after the sun had set since she'd started working at Diva Nation. She needed to get out more. She took a quick glance at his physique as he easily lifted the bulky luggage.

Getting out's not the only thing I need.

She shook her head, clearing it of the thought. Getting any further involved with Mark would be trouble— no matter how much she liked him personally.

Man, it had been a long day, a long drive. A long night.

They checked in with the night clerk, and got their keys. As luck would have it, they had rooms right next to each other. They rode the elevator in companionable silence. Finally, they were each at their respective hotel-room doors.

"Well, I guess this is it." She held out her hand. "Thank you. For the ride, for being a great conversationalist. For everything."

His hand was warm and firm in hers. "I feel like we've been to war together."

She laughed, then bit her lip. "Would a hug be totally inappropriate? Because. I swear, after that car ride, I feel like I'm leaving my best friend here."

He laughed, put down the laptops and his duffel bag, and held out his arms. Putting down her purse, she moved into his arms, hugging him tightly. He smelled good and felt like a billion dollars, giving the perfect hug…just enough arm, not too crushing, not at all reluctant.

She was really, really going to miss him. It was ridic-ulous, after only six hours, but she was going to miss him like crazy.

She was turning to tell him that, she would tell herself later. She wasn't turning to do anything else when she was still in his arms. She just looked up into those sky-blue-gray eyes of his, smiling when he stroked the side of her face. Smiling back at him.

She was still smiling when he leaned down. The two of them were smiling when their lips met. And for a second, it was absolutely perfect—the end of a perfectly awful day with the most wonderful ending imaginable.

Then something changed. Oh, it was perfect—but there was nothing friendly about it.

She felt him crush the hair at the nape of her neck, very gently, with his broad hand, holding her more tightly to him as she let out a soft moan and pressed herself against him. She opened her mouth and felt his tongue brush against her lips, tickling hers. She tilted her head for better access, and sighed right into him. He felt sinfully delicious and tasted like heaven. She clutched at his shoulders, feeling him press her against the door. She didn't care. She wanted as much of him as she could get.

She had no idea how long they stood like that out in the hallway, but it was probably far too long…and it wasn't even long enough. But she heard one of the bags falling over and, startled, she pulled back.

"Wow," Mark said, his breathing uneven. "Just…wow." He stared at her. "You okay?"

She took a deep breath. "I think you shorted out my left temporal lobe."

He laughed, stroking her arms. She took a step back, studying him.

"Do you have any idea how outrageously good you are at that?"

He grinned, tongue in cheek, and leaned against the door frame. "Good manners would say I should be modest right about now," he said, then he grinned devilishly. "But hell, I'm too tired. Yeah, I knew."

"Good grief. You should wear a warning label. Be registered as lethal in most states."

He winked at her. "Just most states?"

"Well…I'm betting you'd probably be okay in Hawaii," she said. "Thanks again."

"You make me laugh," he said, his smile causing her to feel warm all the way down to her toes. "I dig that."

"Who says *dig* anymore? What are you, Austin Powers?" She had to escape. If she stayed out here…

"Why?" He winked. "Do I make you *randy,* baby?"

"You nutcase," she replied. "I dig ya right back."

He sighed. "It was the kissing thing, huh?"

She thought about it. "Actually, it was the car ride. I've never met anybody who could talk about as many non–work related things as you," she said. "It takes a man of true distinction to find Andromeda, debate the finer points of *A Face in the Crowd* and sing all the words to 'Dead Man's Party' in a decent voice."

His eyes lit up, like a kid at Christmas, and his grin was so happy she wanted to drag him into her room and not let him go, possibly ever.

"You keep smiling like that, Tennessee, and I'm going to do things I regret. So let's call it a night." With that—and because she was an utter, stupid glutton for punishment—she gave him one last, quick kiss, then opened the door, dumped her stuff inside and shut the door behind her. Then, she kicked off her shoes and threw herself onto her bed. She heard him hauling his bags into his room next door, and closed her eyes.

Okay, you're an idiot, she berated herself. Kissing that man was like juggling chain saws. Might seem like a cool idea in theory, but if you didn't know what you were doing, you were bound to get hurt.

Still…he was pretty amazing. And of course, gorgeous. And really funny.

And *damn,* that man could kiss.

Suddenly, there was a knock on the door, and she groaned. "Will this day never end?"

She peeked through the peephole…and saw a figure that still managed to look good despite the distortion of the fish-eye lens.

Don't do it. You're tired. You're slap happy. You haven't had sex in two years, she admonished herself. *He works for the enemy. Do. Not. Open. That. Door.*

She saw her hand grab the doorknob, twist it and swing the door open.

"Forget something?" she inquired.

His answering smile made her toes curl.

"You know," he said, "sometimes, regret is healthy for you. Besides, it's been a long time since I've done something somebody's regretted."

Without another word, she grabbed him by the shirt and shut the door behind him. His lips were on her before the dead bolt even shot the lock.

"We must be crazy," Sophie muttered breathlessly against Mark's neck, even as her fingers flew to the buttons on his shirt, undoing them slowly. She wasn't going slowly out of any inherent sexiness…. Passion and exhaustion had made her fingers clumsy.

She knew her brain was too tired to be thinking rationally. Otherwise, she'd acknowledge just how universally stupid this course of action was. She'd driven six hours to get here, after a full day of traveling, and now she had a complete stranger in her hotel room after midnight when she had one of the biggest meetings of her career at, what, nine o'clock the next morning....

She suddenly pulled back to stare at him. Good God, what *was* she thinking? Was she a complete and utter moron?

"Mark..."

He smiled, his eyes aglow. Then he leaned down and devoured her mouth. Her fingers twined into the hair at the nape of his neck. She felt his fingertips dig into her hips, pulling her forward, molding her against what felt like a sizable hardness. She opened her mouth, tasting him, cuddling him at the juncture of her thighs as she pressed her breasts against his chest.

Oh, yeah. A complete and utter moron, indeed, was her last coherent thought.

But a *happy* moron.

He tugged at her until the two of them tumbled onto the queen-size hotel-room bed. For a second, they lay there, kissing softly. It wasn't clawing, or rushed, or even a mad grappling. It was more like coming home. Yes, that was a cliché, but since she'd never really felt it before, even when she *was* coming home to someone...

She wasn't going to think about that now.

He moved from her mouth to her jawline, insistent

kisses against her neck. She gasped a little, and her hands went back to his shirt, finally succeeding in getting the last of the buttons undone. She pushed the shirt away from his chest, letting her palms slide over the taut muscles of his torso. He felt hot, and smooth, and perfect. He was kissing her collarbone, and for a second, she forgot how to breathe.

He reached for the hem of her short-sleeved blouse, and pulled away enough for her to wiggle out of it as he pulled it up over her head. He shrugged out of his shirt, and the lace of her bra was the only thing between the heat of their skin. She sighed against him, rolling him onto his back and straddling him. He reached for her belt buckle as she kissed him, over and over.

This was madness. Utter, fantastic madness.

He had her buckle undone and the top button on her linen pants open, unzipping slowly, and she laughed with sheer abandon. "I never do this," she murmured, wondering if he'd think she was easy. Wondering if it was too late to be wondering about that kind of thing.

Wondering, halfheartedly, if she really cared.

"I never do this, either," he said instead, and he smiled at her, a sugary kind of smile that had her smiling right back before he started kissing her again, deeply, and moving her over on her back. "You are exceptional in all kinds of ways, Sophie Jones."

"And you're wonderful," she said, and meant it. She barely registered the fact that he'd tugged her pants off, leaving them on the floor. Now she was in her underwear and knee-high socks, and he was still in his trousers. "Come here."

He slipped off his trousers and socks and then he was just in boxers, striped white and blue, which for no reason she thought was amusing until she saw the erection tenting the front of the material. She suddenly didn't find anything funny at all. She only felt desire, white-hot and ravenous.

He covered her with his body, kissing her, and she kissed him back passionately. She reveled in the feeling of his fingers combing through her hair, and she clutched at his back.

Then she felt his hand smooth down her shoulder, skim over her rib cage and cup her breast.

"Oh," she gasped, tearing her mouth away from his as the sensation shot through her. After two years, it was almost more than she could bear, complete sensation overload on a global scale.

His hand paused on her, and she could feel the heat of his palm through the lace of her bra. "All right? Are you okay?"

"More than," she murmured, arching her back and pressing more firmly into his hand. He was between her legs, only the thin material of her panties and his boxers between them. "This is… Oh, my."

He pushed once, experimentally, and circled her nipple with his fingers at the same time. She opened her eyes long enough to see him smile, a tender smile, and she almost came undone in his arms.

He leaned down and kissed her again, and she couldn't help it…. She wrapped her legs around his, feeling herself go damp enough to soak her underwear. He had to feel it, too, because she could feel the muscles at his shoulders bunching and heard him groan against her neck as he pressed a hard kiss against her. "You're sure?" he whispered.

"More sure than I've been about anything," she said recklessly. "Please. Please, make love to me."

He pulled back, his blue eyes lit like blowtorches. "I want to, believe me." He paused. "I can't believe I'm asking this, but…you wouldn't happen to have a condom, would you?"

She whimpered. "No. I don't…. That is… I haven't had sex in a long time." And she really, really wanted to rectify that, she thought, staring at the harsh beauty of his face, the absolute perfection of his torso…the feel of him pressing between her thighs.

"Damn it." He rolled off her, and she felt bereft, trying to follow him, but he kept her at arm's length.

"What is it?"

"I don't have a condom, either," he said, his breathing ragged. "I don't do this, like I said, and I don't generally travel with condoms handy."

She felt frustration claw at her, and couldn't help but let out a growl of pain. Even so, a little part of her felt a thrill…glad that he didn't do this all the time. Glad that she wasn't the only one who was out of her mind because of this whole situation. "I'm sorry," she said inanely.

"Why?" Despite the wince of frustration as he rolled onto his side, he then sent her a wistful, lopsided smile that made her heart race. "It's nobody's fault. And I, for one, don't regret a minute of it." He laughed. "Well, okay. I regret not being more prepared."

She rolled onto her back, wondering how long it would take before her blood cooled down and her heart stopped galloping in her chest. She was also not sure how long it would take before she'd be able to get to sleep. *If* she was able to sleep at all tonight.

All at once, a wave of exhaustion hit her. It had been an amazingly long day. She felt as if all the aches of the travel, all the craziness and all the stress that had been creeping up on her for far too long, just hit her like a tidal wave. To her intense embarrassment, she felt a tear creep down her cheek. She hastily wiped it away, but not before he saw it.

"Shh… Baby, what's wrong?"

"It's been such a crappy day," she said, trying to blink hard as more tears followed the first. "And I really, really wanted to make love to you."

To her surprise, he stood up…then pulled the covers back, lifted her and tucked her in, climbing in next to her and spooning with her, his arms wrapped around her comfortingly. She could still feel his erection, nestled against her bottom, and it was all she could do not to whimper and wriggle against him. He had to be hurting with need, as it were, but he spoke to her gently. "Listen, we both wanted it. But it's probably just as well. You've been through a whole lot. I don't even know you, and I know that."

That was the thing, she thought, as she let herself cry onto the pillow, her cheek warming with the heat of the tears. He didn't know her. But damned if he didn't know exactly how to help her feel better at any particular moment.

"I really like you," she said, with a slight catch in her voice. "Seriously. And not because of what we were going to do."

He laughed, and she felt the reverberations through his rib cage. "Sugar, I really like you, too." He nuzzled the back of her neck, and she pressed against him.

She turned around, hearing him groan again as she inadvertently brushed against him. She faced him, stroking his cheek. Then she kissed him, tenderly, deeply…. A thank you, for being such a wonderful man at a time when she needed someone to lean on. It was a new sensation—having someone rescue her.

"What was that for?" he said, resting his forehead against hers.

"Mark McMann," she said, in a teasing, singsong voice, "you're my hero."

He laughed, so she kissed him again…and things quickly got more serious than she'd intended, as they pressed against each other. So close, so *damned* close…

She was the one who pulled away this time, gasping for air, gasping against the furious heat of her body. "Maybe the manager would bring up a box," she said, half-joking.

He spun her around again, pulling her to him. "Go to sleep," he said, and she could hear the words through the gritting of his teeth.

"I'm—"

"Don't say you're sorry. I swear to God, if I have to scour all of San Antonio, I'm going to find a condom and tomorrow night, this is all going to be just the world's longest bout of foreplay. But for right now, I'm holding you until you fall asleep, then I'm going back to my room to dream about all the things I'll do to you tomorrow night. Your perfume's going to haunt me, for starters."

She smiled, letting the warmth of him comfort her. "It's our brand. The Essential Sensuals line." She sighed. "I'm glad to know that this particular scent is as sexy as advertised."

"No work talk," he muttered, and she smiled.

"No work," she said, yawning and burrowing slightly into the covers. She felt his arm tighten around her, and she felt the exhaustion and the emotional roller coaster finally start to slide.

"Sophie?"

"Hrmm?" she half enunciated, feeling the edges of sleep closing in on her.

"Nothing." He kissed her shoulder. "Just go to sleep."

2

MARK WOKE UP IN A HOTEL BED, not surprisingly. It was early, though—he'd forgotten to shut the shades. He must've been more tired than he'd thought.

His hand moved across the pillow, and he heard a startled sigh.

He sat bolt upright.

He wasn't in his room. He was in *her* room. In *her* bed. With the rest of the conference probably filing into this very hotel at any moment.

"Uh-oh," he muttered.

She sat up slowly, took one look at him, and then he could tell from the horrified expression on her face and the way her mouth was opening that she was about to scream. He quickly did the only thing he could think of…covered her mouth with his hand. Her shriek turned into a muffled squeak.

"Hi, I'm Mark McMann. Any second now, you're going to remember me from last night. We drove in together last night, laughing, were both tired, we didn't have a condom…." He smiled without humor as a look of recognition crossed over her face. The look of horror, he noted, redoubled. "Ah, here we go. You remember."

He removed his hand slowly, and she gasped. "You're still here. It's morning, and you're still here."

"In my defense, I was exhausted... Hey!"

She jumped out of bed and bolted past him, dashing to the center of the room, looking as if she were trying desperately to get her bearings. He noticed that she was only wearing panties, and she didn't seem to care in the slightest. "What time is it?"

"Uh..." His brain had shorted out temporarily, seeing that lithe body of hers wearing only a pair of silky-looking bikini-cuts. "Um..."

She looked around at her clothes, then pushed her blouse out of the way of the clock. "Eight o'clock! Crap! *Crap!*" She glanced back at him. "Focus, Tennessee. Grab your clothes and get back to your room! ASAP!"

He blinked. Of course, that had been his plan, before he'd frozen in the headlights, as it were. He'd seen naked women, although they were usually models. And they weren't usually shaped like Sophie. For a short girl, she certainly had...

"Mark!" She snapped her fingers in front of his face. "Not that it isn't flattering, but you've got to wake up, sweetie. Do you really want people to know we spent the night together?"

Those were the magic words. He jumped out of bed, thankful that he was still wearing boxers. He assiduously avoided looking at her and instead did as she said, focusing on grabbing his clothes and pulling them on, tripping back onto the bed as he tugged his pants on both legs at one time.

"Can't you hurry?" he heard her call from the bathroom. The shower was running…. Man, he needed to jump into the shower. He needed to unpack, for God's sake. He needed to get moving…. His boss Simone was probably in the hotel by now, and would probably want to call the staff meeting at 10:00 a.m. or something…. Jeez, he needed to look at his PDA, see if he'd gotten any e-mails; she was all about sending those sneaky e-mails to make sure people were plugged in all day.

He buttoned his shirt hastily, noticing that he seemed to be missing a button…and abruptly remembered how he'd lost it. He went slightly hard and quickly headed off any more thoughts in that direction.

It was just a temporary lapse of reason. People were considered innocent for stuff like murder with just that kind of rationale. Besides, it wasn't as if it were ever going to happen again.

"I'm out of here, I'm really sorry…" he said to the open bathroom door, figuring she was in the shower. "I'll…er…"

He'd what? Call her later? They hadn't even had sex, for pity's sake. And now they weren't ever going to see each other again. That thought caused a little sting, but he'd get over it. So what else could he say?

"Have a good conference," he finished lamely and headed for the door. He looked out the peephole and then opened the door, peering out. Nobody in the hallway. He dug around in his pocket, found his room key and then made a break for it. He got in the room quickly and noticed immediately that the hotel-room phone light was blinking. He had a message. He decided to jump in the shower and get dressed first, before dealing with it. Odds were good it was somebody he didn't want to talk to, anyway…or somebody it would stress him out to know he'd missed. He could just say that he'd slept in or something.

He thought back a minute, thinking of Sophie, naked on the other side of the wall.

Or something.

Finally, in a world's record of getting cleaned up, he collected the message.

"Mark? This is Simone. I think something might be wrong with your phone. I've decided to call an impromptu staff meeting at nine this morning, and I want you there a few minutes early…. I think we need to talk." A pregnant pause. "Yes. We definitely need to talk."

Mark winced, then grabbed his briefcase. He wasn't going to bring his laptop—Simone didn't approve of them in meetings. He was almost out the door when he suddenly found that his phone was missing. He searched for it frantically, cursing a blue streak when it didn't show up. He didn't even have stuff out of his bags, for pity's sake, where could he have…

He winced.

Sophie.

He took a deep breath, glanced at his watch. Eight-forty.

He should leave in five minutes. He prayed that Sophie hadn't rushed off….

He looked down the hallway again, as furtive as a spy, then knocked softly on her door. Then knocked louder.

"Just a minute!"

She opened the door. She looked…well, wet, to be honest, her toffee-colored waves pulled back in a ponytail that emphasized the classic lines of her face. She was wearing glasses, cute wire-rims. She blinked at him as she put an earring in her ear.

"Hi," he said, and without waiting for an invitation, he dashed into her room.

"Um, hi. I'm in a hurry…."

"I can't find my phone," he explained, looking around. She'd done the same thing as he had—dug into her bags for clothes—but otherwise everything was as is. Except for the clothes she'd stripped off last night, which were still in a trail that led to the bed.

Don't think about it, don't think about it….

"Listen, about last night," she said softly.

"No worries," he interrupted. "Really. We were both tired, we weren't really thinking, it just seemed like a good idea at the time…."

"That's not it."

He looked up, finally. She looked near tears.

He tried not to think about how hot she'd been. How very, very much he'd wanted her. How much he still wanted her, come to that. She was amazing, sweet and sexier than anybody he'd met in a long time.

"It's not that bad," he said. "You didn't…"

Before he could say anything else, she flew at him, and he felt that hot, mobile mouth of hers against his. And whatever strange craziness had come over him last night was back again with a vengeance. It wasn't a fluke…wasn't because they were tired, wasn't because they were punch-drunk and lonely.

She still wanted him.

His hands clutched at the small of her back, dragging her up against him…. Then he pulled away. What was he doing? He had a meeting in minutes, and so did she, and what were *they* doing?

Besides, you still don't have a condom.

"I still want you," she breathed. "I know the timing's lousy, and it's probably not anything either of us should do anything about, I mean we're professionals, and…" She stopped. "I'm babbling."

"You hate that," he couldn't help but point out, with a smile, thinking of last night.

"The thing is, I would still love to make love with you. I just thought you should know that." She shrugged, the blush on her cheeks owing nothing to cosmetics.

He reached out and kissed her back, hard, gratifying in the sound of her low moan. "You don't even know how much I still want to make love to you," he ground out finally. "But you're right. The timing, the…"

"It's crazy," she said with a shrug. "In fact, it's stupid. But if I didn't tell you…well. I didn't want you to think that I regretted it, or that it was a mistake."

He was torn. It was stupid, potentially career damaging. As one of the few men in a women-dominated profession, it was dangerous. And it was definitely unprofessional. It would get around. Hell, rumors of him sleeping with women, that were completely unfounded, still surfaced from time to time. And with his promotion coming up...

He sighed. "I'm sorry. You're right—we can't."

She nodded, looking for a moment completely dejected. "I'll help you find your phone."

He saw it suddenly, a silver object, half-hidden by the thrown-back comforter on the bed. "Here it is." He grabbed it and knew he should be out the door, with his briefcase, finding Simone. But the problem was he didn't want to go.

"Have a good conference," she said, echoing his earlier lame goodbye.

He wanted to kiss her...reassure her that neither of them had made a mistake. Or better, tell her to wait for him...that after her meeting and his, after whatever else they had to do today, he'd sneak over and they'd make love till morning, damn the conference, damn everything else.

But he wouldn't do that. And she wouldn't, either. And they both knew it.

He held out a hand. She stared at it for a moment, then shook it firmly.

"It was nice meeting you, Sophie Jones," he said, and regret drowned every word.

Then he turned and headed out the door.

SOPHIE GLANCED AT HER WATCH, then glanced back at the empty stage. After all her fuss to make the morning meeting, she now discovered that the meeting itself had been canceled and replaced with a press conference. Sophie was a bundle of nervous energy, since Mrs. Marion had left a message for Sophie specifically to sit up front at the event.

This could be the announcement we've been waiting for.

She was surrounded by tons of people, all sitting at the various tables set up. Marion & Co. had appropriated the second-largest ballroom, and she would've wagered that everyone at the regional trade show had abandoned their various booths to hear what was being said. Well, okay, the big companies, anyway. All the trade reporters were milling around. She would be able to tell them apart by the hungry, searching look in their eyes, if not by their press badges. They didn't get paid much, poor bastards, but they sure did work hard for the money.

She realized she was glancing around to see Mark. *Not that you're at all eager to see him,* her mind ruthlessly taunted her. She'd thrown herself at him briefly this morning, when she'd gotten her wits about her. She'd been disconcerted by finding a man in her bed, after all this time—and the first thing on her mind was the Marion meeting.

If only that had been on your mind before *you invited him to sleep over last night, you idiot.*

It was strange. Normally, she was all business. But she'd taken one look at gorgeous, godlike Mark Mc-Mann, and most of her sharp-hewn common sense had taken a flying leap out the window.

She shook her head. It probably wouldn't hurt her reputation all that much, all things considered, to sleep with a competitor, but obviously it bothered him. Enough for him to rescind his really wonderful, beautiful, sexy offer from the night before.

The offer that she still would've loved to take him up on.

She closed her eyes, squinched them shut. *No, no, no. Just move on, will you?*

She saw Lily Hunter, Mrs. Marion's second in command, crossing the stage, and sat up. The people who were making all that noise quieted, and they looked up expectantly.

She heard someone approach, turned…and saw Mark, looking out of breath. He smiled at her, and her irritation suddenly melted.

He really is beautiful, she thought. *In a purely masculine way. Like a carved fallen angel.*

She frowned, then pulled out the little notepad that she always carried in its little leather binder. She jotted down: "Fallen Angel. Maybe a new perfume? Or add to the new line of eye shadows?"

He sat down next to her, looking curiously at her note, then at her.

She simply smiled. They weren't supposed to know each other, but here they were. And it wasn't as if they were wearing matching T-shirts that said I Almost Slept With and arrows pointing to each other.

She smiled at the image, and he smiled back, then they both turned to the stage, where Abigail Marion strode, looking like a queen clad in her caramel-colored Yves Saint Laurent suit. She had a smile on her face, the one that seemed to say "I know something you don't know."

Sophie glanced at Mark. She wondered if he knew what was going on, but he seemed puzzled…and a bit more annoyed, she noted.

She squelched a smug smile. *Not as annoyed as you're going to be when you find out that a tiny company like mine has poached a huge account from a big company like yours!*

Sure, she might be in lust with the guy. But business was business.

"I'm glad that so many of you could make it to this announcement, on such short notice," Mrs. Marion said, in a rich, cultured voice. "I am also glad that the Southwestern Cosmetics Trade Show management let us have the ballroom so we could make this brief statement."

You could hear a pin drop. Someone coughed in the back of the room, and Sophie could've sworn she felt everyone wince in unison. They were all riveted.

"Marion & Co. has been fortunate enough to have enjoyed significant growth in revenue in the past few years, dealing in exclusive luxury items for the most discerning shoppers," she said. "We only offer the best products from the absolute, most exclusive providers. We offer several select brands, only the finest. Cosmetics has been one such area."

Now, Sophie thought she could feel the whole room hold its collective breath. She could barely breathe, herself.

"We would like to partner with a cosmetics company to create a new house cosmetics brand…a partnership brand, if you would. It would still retain the cosmetic company's name, and have a distinct identity. But it would carry the weight of Marion & Co.'s seal of approval. The distinct sub brand would only be available at Marion & Co…but I don't need to tell you all what sort of a boost this would be."

There was a buzz of frenetic chatter after this, as the thrum of commentary followed. It would be more than a boost—it would be an absolute windfall for whatever lucky cosmetics company M&C partnered with.

Sophie felt her heart beating a staccato rhythm in her chest. *This is it,* she chanted in her mind. *This is it, the chance we've been waiting for…*

"After a private, relatively secret search, we have narrowed the field of competitors to two."

Sophie's eyes widened.

Wait a minute.

Two?

Whatever gossipy buzz had been traveling through the room ceased as all ears pricked up.

"First…Trimera International, headquartered in New York."

Sophie saw Mark sit up a bit straighter, his eyes gleaming avariciously.

"And second…Diva Nation, from California."

She could hear people muttering "Who?" after Diva Nation was announced. She suddenly felt the overwhelming urge to crow—and an equally powerful urge to make a break for her room before her incognita status disappeared. She got the feeling that by tonight, every single person at the conference would know exactly who she was and who she represented.

'Bout time!

"Congratulations," Mark murmured to her, and she nodded, accepting it. His eyes weren't gleaming anymore. Instead, they studied her…appraising, yet wary.

Mrs. Marion smiled at the shock wave she'd sent through the conference. She was obviously a woman who liked to push buttons, and cause a stir. "To these two companies, I am asking for a series of distinct proposal rounds. Your individual headquarters will be receiving the necessary materials by this afternoon. This brand will be rolling out by the end of next year. Thank you, all of you, for your time."

With that, and with people clamoring out with questions, Sophie felt herself go numb.

"Who the hell is Diva Nation?" a woman next to her asked, sourly. "Mark…heard of them?"

"Yup," he said, looking at Sophie. "They're a sort of underground urban cosmetics brand, out of L.A."

She blinked. She hadn't told him that. He'd somehow…

Of course he knew. She grimaced, and quickly snatched up her things, grabbing her phone as almost an afterthought.

"Yeah, but who the hell are they?" the woman persisted.

Sophie didn't wait to hear what his response was. She just made a beeline for the door.

Mark was right behind her, it turned out. She knew because of the cologne he wore…. It wasn't overpowering, but it was really nice, and suited him to a T. "Wait up," he said.

"I'm sorry, I've got to get going," she said quickly. "It's now going to be a really chaotic conference for me."

"You pulled off a coup back there," he said, and admiration was obvious in his voice. "Did you know they were going to give you a chance at the account? When I gave you a ride?"

She glanced around. People were watching them. More to the point, they were watching *him*. Women couldn't keep their eyes off him, which was hardly a shock. "I thought we weren't going to talk business," she said in a hushed, reprimanding voice.

"That was last night," he murmured. "I think things have changed since then, don't you?"

"They have changed," she said ruefully. "Now, we're direct competitors, not just rivals in the same industry. And we really, really need to not talk anymore."

He was still following her as she walked toward the

elevator bank. After they waited there in silence, he said, "I'm not stalking you. I'm only trying to get to my room."

She drowned again for a second, wallowing in memories of last night…of the two of them. Of his earlier promise to make love to her all night tonight. "No problem," she said, glad her voice managed to sound casual.

The two of them rode the elevator in silence, ignoring the gaggle of sales reps who surrounded them as they managed to get off on earlier floors, all of them commenting bitterly on Trimera getting chosen, and all wondering about Diva Nation. Sophie made sure that her arms covered her name badge. Finally, it was her and Mark alone, on the elevator, headed for the twelfth floor.

"What are you doing for dinner tonight?"

She glanced at him. "Sorry?"

"Dinner. Tonight." He sent her a sidelong glance that practically melted her heart. "I was sort of wondering. I mean, you've got to eat, I've got to eat.…"

She stared at him. "Hello. We're up against each other for this account!" Was the man insane?

He stared at the ceiling of the elevator, contemplatively. "And yet, I still crave food. I imagine at some point, you might feel a little nibbly. So what the hell, we run up the white flag and just have a bite?"

"No, Mark."

"No, you won't be hungry?"

"No, I won't be eating with you!" She couldn't help it, she laughed. "Damn. Either you've got a ton of moxie, or…"

She stopped. *Or he'd reconsidered his stance on sleeping with her.*

Of course. Now that she absolutely could not, in good conscience, sleep with him…he'd changed his mind.

"I'm not sleeping with you," she said bluntly.

Now he smiled back at her, devilishly handsome. "Um…ever?"

She forced herself to keep a straight face. "More than likely. But definitely not as long as we're both in the running for this account."

"Somehow," he said, "I can probably manage to share a meal with you without pushing the dishes aside and just taking you on the table."

The image that conjured up sent shivers of heat along her body. "Don't even joke," she said, hating the breathless edge her voice took on.

"I wasn't really joking," he said.

He was dangerous.

"Stay away from me, Mark," she said. "I really appreciated yesterday…on a couple of levels. And I would've loved to become friends with you. But you've got to see how this won't work."

He took that in silence for a moment, then the two of them headed to their respective rooms. She noticed her hand shaking slightly as she wrested with the card key.

She'd been so close to sleeping with him, she thought, with regret so keen it was painful. Now, she knew that every single ounce of common sense told her that he was off-limits, for good.

He pulled out his wallet, producing a business card that he quickly scrawled something on. "Here," he said.

She stared at it. "What's this for?"

"It's my cell-phone number," he said. "Just in case you change your mind about dinner." He paused. "Or anything else."

She watched as he effortlessly opened his room door and shut it behind him. She finally went into her own room…the card burning a hole in her pocket.

You're not going to call him, she told herself.

Still, she couldn't bring herself to throw the card away.

"ALL WE HAVE TO DO IS TAKE OUT one puny competitor, and the house brand for Marion & Co is ours," Simone said, back at the office in New York. "Now—brainstorm. What do we know about Diva Nation, and how can we knock them the hell out?"

Mark looked at his boss, and then at the VP of marketing, Roger, who was sitting in on the meeting. They were both standing at the head of the large conference-room table, looking puzzled. Well, *puzzled* wasn't the best way to describe it. Simone looked determined, as always, but also somewhat frazzled. Roger looked gob-smacked. The rest of the Trimera team, seated around the broad expanse of table, was somewhere between the two. Except for the resident pit-bull saleswoman, Carol, who looked as if her solution would involve some kind of violent force.

"I cannot believe this. I cannot…frickin'…believe

this," Roger finally said, anger filtering through his obvious surprise.

Simone sighed. "Roger, we've been over this."

"I don't think you realize what a slap in the face this is," he countered, obviously eager to discuss in front of the team what he'd already hashed out with Simone in private. "Marion & Co. has always carried Trimera. We've always had a good relationship with them. Now, they're creating an exclusive house brand, and they're going to pit us against some nobody brand from California?" He looked at Mark. "I thought sales were doing well in that channel! Could somebody please tell me how the hell this happened?"

Carol cleared her throat before Mark could respond. "Account management has reported some problems with the Marion & Co. account," she said, her voice deceptively calm. Her eyes looked fiery and triumphant, though.

"That true, Mark?" Roger snapped.

Mark forced himself not to glare at Carol. "Actually, it's not," he responded, his voice cool. "At least, we may have lost sales volume, but not market share. We're doing fine." He paused. *If you'd read my last three reports, you'd know that.*

Roger brushed off the comment, as Mark knew he would. "So, if we're doing fine, who the hell is Deviant Nation, anyway? And why are they even in this?"

"Diva Nation," Mark corrected. "They're a small independent brand out of Los Angeles. They're getting some decent distribution, though, and their products are getting a good deal of buzz. They're not much now, but if their numbers keep up…"

He drifted off when they all looked at him.

"Is there any pulse you don't keep your finger on?" Simone asked with admiration.

He didn't want to think about how many fingers he'd had on the pulse of Diva Nation…or how much closer he would've gotten, if she'd let him.

"I keep an eye out," Mark said elusively.

"Well. This calls for desperate measures," Roger said in that finicky, snarky tone of his. "Carol—you're my point person. We've got to make sure that this thing runs smoothly."

Mark felt his blood pressure raise slightly. He was tired of being passed over. And, frankly, this one was too damned important. He really liked Sophie, but business was business—and since business was the one thing that stood between him and Sophie, he figured she'd probably understand more than anyone.

"Roger," Mark interrupted, before the man could continue barking out his instructions, "Simone said that she was going to give me the next product launch. You agreed to let me be point on the next proposal. I think that this counts."

The rest of the team was now openly gaping at him. He had to admit, he was a bit surprised, himself.

Nothing ventured, he reminded himself nervously.

"A little crappy product launch is one thing," Roger

said dismissively, although he seemed surprised, as well, that Mark had spoken up. "But after all, you didn't report the sales information to me, and that would've been important."

Mark gritted his teeth.

"Besides, we're going to need more than charm on this," Roger added. "I need somebody who knows product and figures."

Mark tried not to let the obvious insult get his temper too high. "I know the product, and I know the background. Most of all, I know Marion & Co."

Roger smiled indulgently. "Not well enough, obviously, to—"

"If you'd read the last report I sent, you'd know exactly why we're stuck in this mess."

Now the rest of the team was more than gaping—they looked horrified. Being assertive, or aggressive, was one thing. Committing career suicide in public by challenging one's extremely temperamental vice president...well, now, that was something else.

Smooth move, McMann.

"I see," Roger said, in a flat tone of voice that said he was purely pissed off. He glared at Simone, as if it were her fault things had gotten out of hand.

Simone hastily shuffled some papers on the desk, keeping her voice brisk. "You know, I think that a compromise might work. If Carol took the lead, and Mark worked with her, he could bring his competitive knowledge and his familiarity with the account to the table, while she could hone the message and get the product side in line. What do you say?"

Mark sent a silent prayer of thanks that Simone was firmly on his side. She was far more diplomatic, for one thing—and she'd been playing internal politics for years.

"We'll talk later," Roger said sharply, "but since you seem so intent...fine. McMann, you're working with Carol. I'll expect to see preliminary notes by next week. Pull the meeting together. And don't screw this up," he said, with obvious menace in his voice. "I want this one locked down."

With that, he stalked off. The team let out a sigh of relief as Simone instructed them to go back to their desks. That is, everyone except Carol, who was looking both exceptionally arrogant and irritated.

Gonna have a problem with you, Mark noted.

"Mark," she said, "I'll have my assistant pull together the meeting, and I'll get the notes done, as well. Why don't you send me any information you have on Diva Nation and Marion & Co. in an e-mail? Or give me any copies of paperwork you have." She smiled, an echo of Roger's humoring grin. "I'll start working on the actual presentation."

"I'll work with you, Carol," he said, keeping his voice smooth. *Charm,* as Roger had said. "A lot of my knowledge isn't on paper. I'd rather we just work together."

She set her face in a frown. She was a slender woman, with red hair cut in a straight bob, and eyebrows so sculpted they looked chiseled onto her face. She'd had a problem with Mark since the day he'd joined the team. "Mark, can I talk to you for a minute?" she said in a low voice.

He nodded, allowing himself to be pulled aside, knowing that Simone was studying them intently. "Yes?"

She took a deep breath. "Look, it's obvious that Roger doesn't really want you on this project. So why don't you let me do the bulk of the work?" Her eyes were like laser beams in their intensity. "No offense, but I know that this stuff—reports, this kind of leg work—isn't really your strong suit."

He winced. *Remind me again how that's not supposed to offend me.* "I'm curious—what makes you say that?"

"Well, you've never done something like this before," she said, as if it were patently obvious.

"But I've worked on lots of projects," he countered. "Hell, lots of people on the team have asked me for advice. And Simone knows nobody knows competitive info like I do."

She frowned, as if amazed he was still putting up a fight. "Well, you're a sales guy. You don't have the background…"

"I got my MBA two years ago," he said shortly. "In marketing."

She sighed. "You don't know how we work."

It was like battering up against a concrete slab. He sighed. He wasn't going to win if he fought her way— supposed rational arguments, business talk. He only had one choice left.

He leaned forward, smiling…his most winning smile. He made sure he focused his gaze on her as if she were the only woman on earth. It was something they'd always talked about on the catwalk, back when he'd modeled.

She swallowed hard, obviously taken off guard.

"I won't get in your way, Carol," he said, his voice pitched low, almost intimate. "I know that this is a big deal, and you've probably done tons of marketing launches and competitive proposals. I'm only asking for a chance."

She blinked at him. He'd never turned the full force of his charm on her before—he hadn't wanted to waste the energy, and frankly, he always felt a little dirty when he used it this deliberately. Still, he knew the minute she started to waver.

He deliberately pulled his drawl out to a ribbon. "Please," he murmured. "It would mean a lot to me."

She flushed slightly, and looked away, taking a deep breath before looking back at him. "I…I'll need to do most of the work, though," she said, and then cleared her throat so her voice didn't sound so ragged. "And we'll need to make sure that I'm the one that does most of the talking."

"Of course," he said easily. He didn't agree, but he'd tackle that later—he had a *yes* and he wasn't going to mess with it, just as he'd always learned in sales. "We'll set up something tomorrow to touch base, would that be all right? Then get all the details ironed out."

"All right," she said, although she finally sounded a lot less sure of herself. Then she walked away.

Mark gathered his papers together, and Simone walked up beside him. "You are amazing."

He paused, picking up his pen. "How's that?"

"I didn't think anybody could chill out Warrior Princess Carol," she responded, with a light chuckle in her voice. "But if anybody could, it would be you, huh?"

He chose to ignore that. Simone was his boss, and sort of a friend, but her sense of business ethics could get somewhat hazy. "Thanks for standing up for me with Roger," he said instead, focusing on her kindness.

"It's time. I know you're smart, Mark," she said. "You just need a chance, that's all. So—what else do you know about Diva Nation?"

"Not as much as I'd like," he admitted. "They're not very big, but their products are amazing—really outside the box." He smiled slightly, remembering. "I know that they've got a perfumed body lotion that is practically hallucinogenic."

"Really," she said, her voice ripe with speculation. "I probably don't want to know how you know that."

He realized he was letting something slip, and quickly clammed up. "I'll buy their entire product line before I meet with Carol. And I'll know a ton more by tomorrow."

"You know," Simone said carefully, "I couldn't help but notice you had a bit of a connection with that Diva Nation woman—Sophie, her name was. Right?"

"She's a nice woman," Mark said carefully. "And just because we're competitors doesn't mean I need to hate her on sight, does it?"

"I'm merely saying," Simone continued. "She seemed to like you, too. Maybe you could see what you could find out. I'm sure she'd be happy to talk to you on some kind of neutral ground."

Mark felt it again—that dirty, unethical, icky feeling. "Trust me, she's not the type."

"Already tried, huh?" Simone laughed, and in that moment, Mark wished he were anywhere but here. "I might've guessed. You're going to be a great marketing guy, and you're going to knock this one out of the park. You'll be one of the best."

He smiled weakly, then fled. If being one of the best meant using a sweet person like Sophie…

He shook his head. It wasn't as if he had anything with Sophie, and even if he did…well, he wouldn't do anything to jeopardize that, he promised himself. He just wouldn't.

3

SOPHIE GLANCED AT THE CLOCK by her bed. Ten o'clock. Early, by a lot of people's standards. Unfortunately, she knew that sleep would evade her for another three hours, at least. She felt wired, even though she'd deliberately only drunk decaf all day. She'd gotten a good chunk of work done: she had most of the slides ready for the Marion & Co. presentation. She was a little nervous, but more excited—the sign that it was going to go very, very well.

But right now, she wasn't thinking of the presentation. She was thinking, as usual, about Mark McMann.

She pushed her face down into her foam pillow. They'd agreed not to have any contact other than professional—after all, they were in competition, their paths would cross. But they had to be very, very careful, so no one would suspect how close they'd come to...well, getting very, very close. No friendly chats in elevators, no random "bump-into" exchanges in the lobby. Certainly no drinks in the hotel bar.

It also meant she sure as hell shouldn't call him.

She sighed heavily. Even without the competition, she knew they shouldn't get involved in any way, shape or form. Men who looked like him did not under normal circumstances go for women who looked like her, for one thing. And while Sophie knew she wasn't ugly, she wasn't about to pass for a model any time soon. She also knew that he had plenty of women going after him. He probably had no shortage of willing applicants for the position of bed warmer, and no doubt had spent plenty of time with a variety of them. And that type of man wasn't her type at all.

She thought about Troy, her last and longest-lasting relationship. He had been tall, geeky, with blond hair and glasses. He was a finance analyst, and a good one. They'd met in the MBA program at the University of California, San Diego. In her case, it had been love at first sight. They'd been friends first, but she'd always known they'd shift over to lovers.

What she had not known was they should've stayed friends. She'd nearly smothered in all that comfort and compatibility. And she had to admit, she'd been shocked when he'd said the same thing, just before he'd broken up with her. She'd been the best study-buddy he'd ever had, but he just couldn't see himself marrying her.

Not that you want to marry Mark.

She flipped over. She ought to get up and do something. Clean something. Maybe do some more work, even though she doubted it would be usable, what with her mind highballing as it was at a million miles an hour. She really ought to start that meditation that Lydia had raved about. She ought to do *something*.

Flashback to Mark, pressing her into the bed at the hotel…his weight, his strength, the gentleness of him covering her. How there had only been thin layers of cotton between the two of them and one night of what she felt sure would be unforgettable bliss.

She shivered uncontrollably.

You are insane!

She only barely realized she'd picked up her cell phone and dialed his number.

"Mark McMann," he said, sounding tired.

She stared at her phone, aghast. *What are you doing?*

"I'm so sorry," she said quickly. "I didn't mean…"

"Sophie?"

"Is it too late for me to call?" She winced. "Certainly, it's too late for me to call. You're on the East Coast. It's, what, one o'clock in the morning? Listen, I'll—"

"Don't hang up." He chuckled, and she reveled in the sound, wrapping around her like mink. "I'm glad you called. And don't worry, you didn't wake me. Strangely enough, I couldn't sleep."

She closed her eyes, picturing him next to her. "Funny. Neither could I."

"You know, I can hear the smile in your voice," he pointed out. "It's nice."

She felt like a teenager, talking to a boy for the first time. Her hormones were probably off the Richter scale. "You know, of course, that this is utterly crazy."

"It's one o'clock in the morning. Nobody knows how crazy this is more than I do."

She laughed. "Did you want to talk about anything in particular?"

"No." Now she heard the smile in his voice, and she trembled lightly in response.

"Well…how was your day?"

"It sucked," he said, surprising another laugh out of her. "But it's gotten exponentially better in the past five minutes. Yours?"

"Marginally better. I got a lot of work done today." She winced. "Which, of course, I shouldn't talk to you about at all."

"I wasn't going to ask."

"Yes, but it's stuff like this that makes it even more necessary for us *not* to talk to each other."

"We managed to avoid talking about work for six hours. In a car, no less," he pointed out.

"So, what, we manage to do that for the rest of our lives?" she asked, then winced again. "Not that I'm implying… Oh, hell."

"I'm not reading into that," he said, even though she could tell from the tone of his voice that he wasn't scared off by her innocuous comment. He knew what she meant, she thought, relieved. Sort of. "My point is, we can talk *tonight* without touching on any taboo subjects."

She felt a mischievous grin cover her face. "Is sex a taboo subject?"

There was a pause, and she felt the grin replaced by a blush. What was *wrong* with her? She'd never acted like this with any of her boyfriends, for pity's sakes! Much less a complete stranger!

Not that *much of a stranger,* she reminded herself…and her pulse raced.

"Nope. Sorry," he said, and she felt herself take in a breath, even though she hadn't realized that she'd been frozen. "All the blood left my brain for a second. I had to lie down."

She let out an explosive burst of nervous laughter, a stress relief. "I'm already in bed," she said.

"Really." His voice was rich with speculation. "Well, that's another coincidence. So am I."

"So, here we both are. In bed," she said, wondering even as she said it where she was going with it. This was ridiculous, she knew it.

Yet she couldn't bring herself to hang up. To tell him to hang up.

"Thinking of each other," he said.

"Three thousand miles apart," she added.

"Hmm. Well, that's a good thing, right?" His voice was soothing, comfortable. "That shows it's not just physical."

"Although, we are both in bed. And probably both thinking about sex with each other."

Did she just say that?

He snorted. "That only shows we're not *dead,* honey girl."

"I know this is dumb, but I do miss you," she admitted, closing her eyes. "But I don't know how that's possible. I don't even know you. How could I miss you?"

"You know me better than you think," he said. "But I've got an idea. If we're going to miss each other, we might as well get to know each other better."

"What'd you have in mind?"

"Twenty questions," he said, and she laughed in delight. "First off—what are you most scared of in the world?"

She thought about it, winced. "Snakes. You?"

"Have to say, I'm not too fond of heights. What is your favorite flavor of ice cream?"

"Ben & Jerry's Karamel Sutra," she said promptly. "Man, I could go for a pint of that right about now."

"Me, I'm a huge chocolate fan," he said, and unbidden, she got the mental picture of herself, painted with chocolate...and him licking it off. "Double dark chocolate, with hot fudge."

She shook her head. "My turn. Desert island question—name three famous people you want to be stranded with, and why?"

She could hear a rustling over the cell-phone line and imagined him rolling over in his bed as he answered her questions. She kicked off her own covers, even though it was fall, and her house still held a slight chill, despite being in Southern California.

They ran the gamut for the next hour—books and concerts, college, childhoods. She finally yawned, glancing at the clock. "Oh, man, it's eleven-thirty. You're going to be exhausted tomorrow," she said, feeling the creeping edges of guilt hit her.

"Don't worry. It was worth it," he said with a slight yawn. "I like talking to you, Ms. Sophie Jones."

She smiled, cradling the phone to her ear. "I like talking to you, too. We don't want to do this again, of course, but it was nice."

"One last question?"

"I suppose…but then you've got to get some sleep, mister." She made her voice mock-stern, then giggled.

There was a long pause. "Could you describe your bed to me?"

Her breath caught. "My bed?"

"'Cause I've been picturing you in it for the past hour and a half. I've got you down…but I'm wondering if the bed is going to match my mental picture of it."

She felt a flush cover her body, culminating in heat between her legs. She cursed herself for it. "It's a queen-size bed," she said. "The sheets are jersey…T-shirt material. Very soft and smooth." She ran her free hand over them, feeling the texture beneath her fingertips. "Very…inviting."

She could almost hear his body tense. "Really," he drawled.

"I've also got a pretty thick comforter. Lilac colored. And about a million pillows." She let that sink in. "I'm lying on top of the covers, incidentally."

He groaned, and she couldn't help it…she grinned. "Thanks," he said, and his tone sounded a bit strangled. "That completes the picture nicely."

"Just curious, but what do you picture I'm wearing?"

"Well, I don't know what kind of clothes you own," he said, "so I have to admit, I'm picturing you naked."

Her nipples tightened. "Right back atcha," she said.

"Easy enough," he said. "I sleep au naturel, anyway."

She felt her heart start to hammer. "I remember how hot you get when you sleep," she whispered, then tried to laugh, to lighten the mood. "I could've toasted marshmallows."

"I remember how you feel when you sleep," he said, his voice low and warming. "Smelling your hair. Tucking you up against me."

"I remember how you touched me," she said, and absently smoothed her own hand over the silky material of her nightgown. "I can practically still feel your hands on me."

She heard him take a deep breath, and she could almost whimper with wanting him.

"I have to see you again," he said, his voice ragged.

She closed her eyes. Just like that, reality crashed in on her.

"Mark, we can't," she reminded him. "You know why we can't."

"But I've been thinking about that," he said slowly. "We're two fully grown, conscious, conscientious adults. I don't see why the one thing has to influence the other."

She felt the delicious heat that had been crawling through her dissipate, like a cloud of steam. "You mean, you don't see why our having sex should be at all related to our being business competitors?" she said, her voice laced with irony. "You're absolutely right. It's not like we'll be going at it on the conference table at Marion & Co., after all."

"You can make fun of me all you like," he drawled, "but it's true. What business is it of theirs, if we're involved?"

"Involved," she said slowly, wondering at the word. Was that what they were?

"All I'm saying is, I can't stop thinking about you. I'm starting to realize I don't want to."

Sophie sighed.

He had a history of charming people, she remembered. She also remembered the way he'd offered her a ride—and then had tried to pump her for information.

She wanted to trust him, wasn't sure she should.

"I think about you, too," she admitted.

"Well, then…"

"And then I think about how important all this is. To my company. And my business."

She heard him sigh over the line. "There's more to life than business, Sophie."

"I know that," she said, in a little snappish voice, then she sighed. "So—are you going to ask to be reassigned?"

"What?" The shocked tone of voice would've made her laugh if it weren't so painful. "Why would I do that?"

"To make sure there's nothing in our way," she said, then as gently as possible, she repeated, "there's more to life than business, after all."

A slow pause, then another sigh. "Point taken."

She felt a little dip in her stomach. Belatedly, she knew it was disappointment.

"We'd better not do this again," she said softly. "This…or, you know. The other."

"You're probably right." And the regret was obvious in his voice. "Good night, Sophie Jones."

"Good night, Mark McMann," she said, then clicked off her phone.

It was the smart idea, she knew that for a fact.

So why do I feel like crying?

MARK HADN'T SPOKEN TO SOPHIE since her late-night phone call, two weeks prior. He'd agreed to keep things professional. She was right: they both did have a lot at stake. But this was professional—this was business. Mrs. Marion had called both rival companies and invited them to a dinner meeting in San Francisco.

"I realize this is unorthodox, but I wanted to meet with all of you and lay down some of the parameters of the competition, as it were," Mrs. Marion said, sitting at the head of the table with all the confidence and authority of a Mafia don. Or donna, Mark thought.

Mark sat there with his boss, Simone, and Carol, who had not been won over by his persistence and charm despite his concerted efforts. In fact, she openly resented the fact that Mark was there at all.

Too bad, he thought, sending her a polite, sweet-tea-and-Southern-charm smile that she returned weakly. *In the end, this account's mine, sweetie.*

Then he looked across the table, and his smile faltered.

The only person representing Diva Nation was Sophie, putting her at a distinct disadvantage. She was flanked by competitors, and while she wasn't exactly buckling under the strain, it was obvious that she was uncomfortable. She was assiduously avoiding looking at him, for one thing…. Something Mark was afraid the rest of the table would pick up on.

Not that he and Sophie had done anything, he assured himself. Not that they were *going* to do anything. That thought brought a bit more regret than comfort. But if she kept acting weird, he was afraid they'd assume that something had already happened. Especially after Simone's parting comment to him after the last trade show.

"The competition will have two phases, one at the National Cosmetics Trade Show in Las Vegas, and the second here in Marion & Co.'s home city of San Francisco," Mrs. Marion said smoothly. "While presentation is going to be important, I want emphasis on knowledge of the target market. And I want to be wowed, ladies and gentleman. If I'm not…" She shrugged, her demure smile hiding what Mark knew were barracuda-sharp instincts. "No one *has* to win this competition, necessarily. Your two companies are the best of the best, as far as I'm concerned, for what we're trying to accomplish. But if I don't get something that will knock my socks off, then I won't award the contract to either of you. Those are the ground rules."

Mark watched as that sank in with his colleagues.

Sophie nodded somberly, causing one of the tendrils of hair held back by a barrette to fall forward, curling slightly around her jawline.

He felt his mouth go dry, and quickly took a sip of water. *Stay focused, McMann. She's a wonderful woman, no question—but business is business.*

It wasn't fair, though. It simply wasn't fair.

"Trimera has been doing business with companies like yours for the past thirty years," Carol chimed in, her tone just this side of smug. "I'm sure we'll be able to present you with something satisfactory."

Sophie's gaze darted to Carol, the slightest hint of a frown crossing her face before she smoothed her expression out.

Mrs. Marion caught that, as well. "And what about you, Sophie? This is a big step for your company. Think you're up to the challenge?"

Sophie didn't answer immediately, studying the broiled chicken on her plate instead of speaking. When she did, her voice was calm and clear. "I think that sometimes, big companies can be out of touch with what people really want," she answered carefully. "I know that we're small…but I also know that we're much closer to the target. Being small gives us a distinct advantage."

Mark thought he heard Carol scoff quietly on his right. Simone simply smiled, even though her eyes were twinkling shrewdly. "Of course, that depends on the target. If you're targeting a more youthful market—I'm guessing you're in your twenties, if you don't mind my speculating on your age?" She didn't even pause for Sophie's response to that gibe. "You'll understand that younger generation. You'll be able to make the wild and crazy marketing that they seem to plug into."

"Although," Carol added, "Marion & Co. has a slightly older and more affluent demographic."

Bam. Like a one-two punch, Simone and Carol had managed to imply that Sophie was too young and inexperienced to handle this sort of account, and that she could only market to teenagers who shopped in supermarkets. It was like watching a contract hit.

Sophie didn't even bother concealing her frown this time. "That's not what I meant—"

"And you do have a lot of novelty products," Carol added sweetly. "Those really are adorable. What's that one…your Caliente lip gloss? Very trendy."

Now, Mark was getting annoyed on Sophie's behalf. They weren't letting her get a word in edgewise, and he knew, personally, that she probably wasn't working on a lot of sleep. Her eyes flared, and he had the feeling this was about to get ugly in a hurry—which was probably what Mrs. Marion had in mind to begin with. He could see Mrs. Marion presiding over the proceedings with a Cheshire-cat grin. She obviously liked seeing how people could react under pressure.

He suddenly hated seeing the pressure being exerted on Sophie. Not that he owed Sophie anything, he thought quickly. But his mama hadn't raised him to watch a girl get bullied, in any circumstances.

"Caliente. That's the lip gloss that has red pepper and chocolate, right?" he asked, his voice a shade too loud, effectively cutting across the polite verbal knife-fighting happening at the table.

Now all the women at the table turned to look at him—even Sophie. She nodded, her expression slightly puzzled.

"That's selling really well right now, I understand," he said, ignoring Carol's glare. "The lipsticks and glosses that have an ingredient that causes lip swelling—mint, pepper, that sort of thing—is right on target, for any age group. Especially for women who don't want to shell out money for collagen injections."

Now all the women except Mrs. Marion were frowning at him, including Sophie. Which made no sense, since he was trying to help *her* out.

"I haven't had the chance to actually study Diva Nation's product line," he said, addressing Mrs. Marion, since she was the only one at the table who didn't seem put out with him. "But obviously, you can bet that I will. Really closely."

Mrs. Marion laughed, delighted. "Well, Sophie, it looks like you're in for a fight. Are you up for it?"

Mark looked over at Sophie, whose heated glare could probably melt an iceberg. "I never back down from a fight," she said in a tone appropriate for a blood vendetta.

What the hell did I do? He frowned. Apparently, no good deed went unpunished.

"Neither does Trimera," Carol put in, her tone equally fierce.

Mark shot Carol an annoyed look. Yes, they were competitors, but did she have to be so stupidly blunt about things? She was simply throwing gas on the fire.

"I'm well aware of Trimera's business practices," Sophie replied smoothly, and her tone made sure that everyone knew the comment was derogatory.

Mrs. Marion sat up straighter at that remark, still smiling.

"Our head chemist and product designer used to work for Trimera," Sophie added, taking a sip of water to punctuate her sentence.

"Really?" Simone's tone was surprised. Mark was surprised, himself. However, they were in marketing—and marketing never met the chemists. They dealt with the products afterward. "What made him decide to leave?"

"*She* decided to leave," Sophie said, "because she was asked to."

"You mean she was fired?" Carol interjected.

Now Simone and Mark both glared at Carol, who was oblivious, too intent on trying to insult Sophie to realize she'd screwed up. *Smooth*, Mark thought. He hoped Simone would report Carol's obtuse behavior back to Roger.

"She was downsized," Sophie said without emotion, as the waiter took their plates away. "Apparently, she didn't really fit in with Trimera's vision anymore for product development. While it wasn't stated overtly, they thought perhaps her products were geared toward too *mature* an audience."

Mark blinked a moment, floored that Sophie had so neatly turned the tables on them. She'd gone from being a young, inexperienced kid representing the teen market to a champion of the underdog, who obviously was fired because Trimera thought she was too old to develop cutting-edge cosmetics. If Marion & Co. wanted somebody trendsetting, they had Diva Nation.... And if they wanted someone who was mature, they *still* had Diva Nation. It also cast some doubt on Trimera's business practices—especially if they were willing to fire people who were too old. Hints at age discrimination, which he knew would not sit well with Mrs. Marion.

Beautiful, Mark thought absently, as Sophie smiled serenely. Just beautiful. Sophie was playing them like a concert pianist.

He supposed he ought to be more upset about the whole thing. After all, Sophie *was* the competition here. But at the same time, he wasn't a fan of crushing people who never stood a chance in the first place. And she'd made damned sure that Trimera would not write her off.

Carol, he noticed, was seething. Simone was only frowning, the slightest pucker in her otherwise inscrutable facade. Which he knew, from experience, meant that she was pretty angry as well, but knew enough not to show it.

Yup. It was going to be an interesting competition.

Mrs. Marion obviously felt the same way he did, because she looked practically gleeful. "I think we all understand each other, here," she said, rubbing her hands together. "Nothing like some healthy competition to bring out the best products, I always say. I can't wait to see what you come up with. Shall we order dessert?"

"I'll just have coffee," Carol said sourly.

"A latte," Simone countered. "Decaf."

Mrs. Marion looked at Sophie. "Tell me I don't have to indulge on my own," she said.

Sophie smiled, the edge of anger that had frosted her expression finally melted. "I never say no to dessert," she replied. "And the Double Chocolate Suicide *did* look tempting. But I couldn't possibly eat the whole thing on my own. It was huge."

"I'll split it with you," Mark said. "I love chocolate."

Sophie grinned. "I know."

They smiled for a split second, then Mark quickly realized their gaffe. All the women stared at him—then at Sophie. Sophie, he noticed, looked aghast.

He shook his head. "My love of chocolate is legendary on the trade-show circuit," he said lamely. Carol looked shocked. Simone looked smug. Mrs. Marion— well, her expression was one of amused inscrutability.

Oh, hell.

"Would you excuse me?" he said. "I have to make a quick phone call."

He left, cradling his phone in his hand until he was safely in the hallway. Then he cursed himself under his breath. He didn't need to make a phone call. He only needed a moment to think the situation through.

It was a tiny comment. Practically innocent.

Simone was going to have a field day with that one innocent remark, he just knew it.

Of course—if they assume you're sleeping with her already, you might as well go ahead and do the crime you're being punished for.

For the first time that night, he felt an anticipatory smile cross his face.

"HOW COULD YOU BE SO STUPID?" Sophie muttered to herself for the fiftieth time.

She was sitting in her hotel room, mentally reviewing the dinner meeting. It had all been going so well. She'd been professional, but she hadn't backed down. She'd shown them that she meant business. Then, with two little words, she'd managed to portray herself as a floozy—somebody who was obviously too close to the competition.

"How else was I supposed to know that Mark liked chocolate?" she said, covering her face with a pillow and groaning.

For somebody who prided herself on her professionalism, she was doing a damned poor job of maintaining it when it came to Mark McMann.

The worst part was it was all her fault. If only she hadn't called him… If only she'd stuck to her instincts, kept it strictly business…

Oh, who are you kidding? The only thing you're regretting right now is the fact that you don't have more to feel guilty about.

And there it was, staring her baldly in the face.

She still wanted Mark McMann. Yes, it was foolhardy: he was a competitor; she was a professional; there was a whole litany of reasons why she shouldn't get involved with him. But the bottom line was she liked the way he made her feel.

He's charming. That's his best weapon, her business instincts warned her. But her body was not listening to her common sense. It was more attuned to the siren call of his southern drawl, the way his blue eyes pierced through her like a hot knife through butter.

Damn, but she wanted him. Even after tonight's fiasco. *I've never wanted anyone the way I want him.*

There was a knock on her hotel-room door. She frowned, wondering who it was at this hour. She opened the door cautiously.

Mark was standing there, looking over his shoulder. "Sophie," he said, his voice a low murmur. "Can I come in?"

She nodded, more out of surprise than anything. He hurried inside, closing the door behind him.

"Don't worry," he reassured her. "Nobody saw me come in here."

He shouldn't be here, her instincts kicked up again. *Get him out, before you do something even more stupid.*

"What are you doing here?" she asked instead.

He stared at her, silent, for a long moment.

"You know why I'm here."

She swallowed hard. "Yeah. I guess I do."

It was crazy. Beyond crazy. But she knew exactly why he was there.

She knew, because she felt the exact same way.

She went to the minifridge, getting out a bottle of wine she'd purchased with the intention of drowning her embarrassment. "Wine?" she offered, her voice breaking slightly.

He nodded. She poured the ruby-red liquid, her hands trembling slightly. She jumped when his large hands covered hers. "Allow me," he said smoothly.

She let him take over, feeling a sensation of unreality wash over the whole situation. When he handed her a glass, she took a quick, large sip.

"Are you all right?" he asked in a deep, low voice.

She chuckled, her laughter sounding more hysterical than carefree. "Oh, I'm fine," she responded. *Just as long as I don't think too clearly.* She took two more large swallows of the wine, then put the glass down on the dresser. "So, how do you want to do this?"

He frowned. "Do what?"

"This. Us," she said, making a vague sweeping gesture with her hands that encompassed him, her…and the bed.

He studied her, and she squirmed under his attention. "Come here," he said, keeping his voice soft, as if he were approaching a wounded animal.

She took a deep breath, then stepped toward him.

No turning back now.

He took her into his arms, his body feeling hot and hard and fantastic against hers. But to her surprise, he only stroked her arms and her back. He didn't kiss her, much as she wanted him to. She was trembling, and absently she realized it had nothing to do with desire—and everything to do with fear, at what she was doing, and what she might be ruining.

"You don't have to do this, you know," he murmured against the top of her head, pressing a soft kiss against the crown of her hair. "You don't have to do anything that makes you feel uncomfortable."

She curved against him, her arms wrapping around his waist and holding him tight. For a second, conscience warred with desire.

"It's different when we're…you know. Actually in it," she said slowly, pulling away from him enough to look into his eyes. His face was etched with obvious strain—and an overwhelming tenderness that almost took her breath away. "When I think about you, and the night we almost—you know—it's the easiest decision in the world to make."

He stroked her back, small, lazy circles that made her blood warm. She felt her nipples peak in a rush, and her breathing went shallow. "But…?" he prompted, his voice taut.

"But then I think about everything else," she countered. "I think about what we're doing, and what could happen. And I wonder if I'm making the biggest mistake of my life."

He sighed, then sat on the edge of the bed, tugging gently until she sat next to him. He kept an arm around her, and she felt ridiculously comforted by it. She gave into the urge, and rested her head against his broad shoulder. "And what are you afraid is going to happen?" he continued.

She closed her eyes, picturing the worst. "I'll screw up the account," she said softly. "Someone will find out. Mrs. Marion will think I'm not taking it seriously. I'll get Diva Nation tossed from the running because I look like I lack ethics."

"You don't lack ethics," Mark quickly protested. "We haven't shared any secrets, for God's sake!"

"I know. But I also know that, if you asked me, I might let something slip," she admitted, her voice shaking.

He processed that silently, and she wondered if he understood how big a concession that was—especially from someone like her, whose business was her life.

"I would never ask you," he said. "I know I might've tried to charm you, a while ago, but this is different. Hell, I've never felt anything like this before."

"I know," she said. "It's not even like we have a relationship. Who would believe that we just wanted each other so much, business had nothing to do with it?"

He sighed again. "If I hadn't experienced it myself, I probably wouldn't believe it, either," he admitted.

"So why are we doing this?" she asked helplessly.

When she opened her eyes, his face looked haunted—tortured. "Sophie, I never meant to hurt you."

She quickly kissed his jaw, causing the muscles beneath her lips to bunch. "Shh," she breathed. "You asked how I felt. I didn't tell you to make you feel guilty."

"And yet," he said, laughing bitterly, "that's exactly how I feel."

She silenced him by kissing his neck, then she felt her heart start to beat faster, her stomach tightening with desire. She felt her hands inch lower, her fingertips dancing over the hard planes of his abdomen. "You're not making me do anything," she said, and she gave in to temptation. She shifted her fingers lower, brushing over his erection, which sprang fully to life beneath her touch.

"You're not making this easier," he said through gritted teeth. "Sophie, I don't want to do anything that you're going to regret later."

She paused, her hands perilously close to his waistband. "I don't want to do anything that I'm going to regret later, either," she said, desire battling against uncertainty.

She knew what was going to win.

"So what do we do now?" she breathed, her blood pounding hot and heavy in her chest.

His hand stroked her back, and his other hand cupped the side of her face. His face was the picture of perfection, harsh and gorgeous and full of passion.

"Would you regret it," he asked, his voice fierce, "if we never slept together?"

That surprised her, but she knew that he was just trying to convince her…to convince them both. She thought about it, then finally made her decision.

"Yes," she said. "Yes, I would."

"No one will find out," he said, almost to reassure himself as much as her. "And we won't do this again, not if it makes you unhappy, or if you do wind up feeling regret. This won't affect the competition, or any business matters, or anything else whatsoever." He kissed along her jawline, and her pulse danced beneath his attention, causing his words to simply float in her mind, almost meaninglessly. "It's a risk, Sophie. But I think it's one worth taking."

"Oh," she murmured, as his hands cupped her breasts. "Yes…"

"I won't do anything to hurt you," he promised her. "No matter what this is, I swear I won't do anything to hurt you."

She arched her back, releasing herself back onto the bed. She started to unbutton his shirt with trembling fingers.

"I know you won't," she said, and gave herself over.

"I JUST WANT YOU," he said, saying the thought that was blazing through him like electricity. "I want you so damned much…."

She leaned up and kissed him again, and this time there was nothing confused or tentative about it. Her lips teased at his, even as her hands tugged his shirt off. He swept his tongue into her mouth, tickling against hers, and she moaned, savoring the taste of him. They broke apart long enough for him to take off her blouse, and he kissed at the lacy edges of her bra as she sighed with pleasure and tugged off her skirt, leaving her only in matching midnight-blue lingerie. He growled with approval.

"Pants," she said to him, undoing his fly.

They made quick work of his pants, socks, shoes and boxers. She was stretched across the chintz cover, her pale skin looking like cream against the lingerie. Her eyes blazed with invitation, her curls tumbling wildly about her shoulders.

She was the most amazing woman he'd ever seen. He reached for her like a starving man, all other thoughts leaving his head in a rush. He kissed her eagerly, wanting to taste all of her—her shoulders, the hollow behind her elbow, the slight indentations of her ribs. She was breathing in sharp pants, her short fingernails clawing delicately against his back, stroking him to incoherence. He leaned down, taking off her panties, and finding the matching curls between her thighs. He reached in, feeling her already damp and waiting for him. He kissed her hips, then her legs, before stroking a quick lick at the juncture between her inner thighs. The surprise of his motion quickly made her clench and tighten against him, involuntarily. His erection throbbed in response. Insistent, he spread her legs apart gently, before sweeping in to taste her, his tongue lightly delving until he found her clit.

She let out a moaning sob, her legs finally relaxing

and opening wider for him. He spread out on the bed, working only her clit with his tongue as he gently pressed one finger into her opening, feeling a wave of wetness. She was insanely responsive, her sounds of desire only stirring him more. He worked more intently, until he felt her stir beneath him, twisting.

He lifted his head. "Anything wrong?"

"No," she said, and she was wearing a mysterious smile he'd never seen on her before. He was intrigued, but before he could pursue the thought further, he noticed she was contorting herself to be nearer to him…that strawberry mouth of hers tantalizingly close to his erection. He still had a finger inside of her when she took him between her lips, stroking the tip of him with her tongue, and the snug pressure of her mouth was matched by a clenching wetness around his finger.

He moaned, returning to her, his tongue matching hers until he thought they'd both explode from it. Her moans caressed his feverish skin, pulling at him, even as her hips bucked beneath his lips. He finally pulled away.

"I need you," he said, his voice grating with desire. "I need to be inside you."

"Yes," she moaned.

He got a condom, his own hands shaking with his need, finally putting the thing on and reaching for her. He didn't mean to rush, but she was already slick with her own wetness, and he felt her muscles tighten around his cock as he buried himself in her. "Oh, Sophie," he muttered harshly.

"Yes," she said, wrapping her legs against his waist. "Deeper. Please, deeper."

She felt like heaven…or the best sin in hell. He was mindless with it, the pure pleasure of it. He didn't want to rush, wanting to savor the feeling for as long as he could. He withdrew slowly, his moan of pleasure mixing with hers as she twisted her hips sinuously and her legs pulled him back, drawing him inexorably deeper. She clawed at him, clutched at him, until he could no longer be slow, couldn't hold back. He pushed deeper into her, his tempo increasing until they almost seemed like one person, the definitions of themselves blurred out of focus by the sheer heat of desire.

"Mark!" she screamed, and he could feel her body contract around his, milking him, shocking him. His body responded by bucking against her, wanting to bury himself in her as completely as possible.

"Yes," he shouted back, his release slamming through him. He clutched at her hips, pumping into her with breathless abandon.

She clung to him throughout, and her responding *"Oh, oh, oh…"* echoed the second wave of her orgasm.

When it was finally over, he collapsed on top of her, mindful enough to be sure he didn't crush her. He couldn't believe it—how it felt, the whole experience. He didn't have the words, and for him, that was shocking in and of itself. So he pressed gentle kisses against her shoulders, nuzzling her, wishing that he had something better to do, to say, to describe how he was feeling.

"Mark?" she whispered.

He pulled himself away enough to look at her. Her eyes were luminous, her face placid. "You okay?" he whispered back, pushing a stray curl out of her face.

She smiled back, full of invitation and happiness and desire, shocking him. His body, which he felt had surely shorted out after such an intense experience, started the first stirrings of desire. *So soon?*

"This," she murmured, kissing him as if to punctuate her point, "is why I said yes."

He nodded. "And that's why I wanted you to," he responded.

"Mark…in case we never do this again," she said, and the very words caused a pang in his chest, "we'd better make tonight worth it."

He rolled off her, but refused to release her, stroking at her sweat-moistened skin with his fingers.

"I'll do my best," he promised, and then proceeded to do exactly that.

4

"YOU'D BETTER LET ME DO ALL the talking," Carol reminded Mark for the fortieth time.

Mark sat in a large conference room at a hotel in Vegas, getting ready for the first big Marion presentation. Carol, when not reminding him that she was the one in charge of the presentation or letting him know "how particularly important this meeting is," was muttering over her slides, practicing as if she were some kind of Shakespearean actress. Despite his best efforts, she'd managed to veto most of his suggestions and had what was possibly the world's most boring presentation. She'd only made the barest of mentions as to what sort of products they'd be designing for Marion & Co., focusing more on showing Marion & Co. that Trimera traditionally sold well for them.

Which wasn't the point at all.

She was allowing him there to keep her promise to Roger and Simone, which irritated the hell out of him. Still, he'd prepared as diligently as he could. He'd even developed a short bullet-point presentation of his own in case he somehow got the opportunity to speak. *Say, if someone decided to drop a house on Carol.*

He grinned. It was unkind to think, but after all her dismissive remarks, he didn't really care too much.

Carol and he were early at arrive to the conference room. The huge cosmetics convention was being held at the Monte Carlo, a posh hotel on the strip in Las Vegas. The room was elegantly appointed, and they were still setting up. He saw Mrs. Marion's assistant—Lily, if he recalled correctly—placing easels on either side of the room, one labeled Trimera and the other labeled Diva Nation.

Stupidly, his pulse picked up.

Maybe it's just as well I'm not speaking today.

He had promised Sophie that their last encounter would not affect the competition between their two businesses whatsoever. He was intent on keeping that promise. What he hadn't known then was how much he'd be thinking of her when they weren't together.... And how distracting thinking of her could be. The slightest thing would set him off into a fugue of fantasy. The midnight-blue shade of one of their skin-care boxes reminded him of her lingerie. The slight waft of sandalwood and rose from a candle in a store left him reeling with the memory of the scent of her hair. He'd itched to call her, even though he'd promised that they would have no more contact until after the competition was over. He'd only been thinking to comfort and re-assure her.

He'd had no idea what sort of impact their night together would have on *him*.

"Can I get you two anything?" Lily, Mrs. Marion's second in command, asked both him and Carol, interrupting his thoughts. "We're bringing in refreshments, but if you want water or a soda or anything, I'll be happy to get them. Oh, and will you be needing help with your laptop, hooking it up to the projector?"

"No," Carol said irritably, and to Mark's chagrin, she actually waved Lily away with her hand in a dismissive motion. He noticed Lily's eyes narrow for a second before pasting her smile back in place.

"Thanks, Lily," he said quickly, but she was already gone.

"You're going to have to watch it," Mark cautioned Carol, causing her to shoot him a look of annoyance. "Lily Hunter isn't some nobody secretary you can dismiss. She's important." In fact, that small sign of disrespect might cost them dearly. He'd need to make it up to Lily later, he reminded himself.

Carol shrugged, completely unapologetic. "I'm trying to concentrate…."

"They won't care," Mark said bluntly. "All the stuff about how well our products have sold in their stores? They're not going to give a damn, so don't sweat those numbers. We've got bigger issues here."

Carol frowned at him. "You may be director of sales, but I've been in marketing and growth for twice as long as you've been with the company," she said, and he knew what Lily must feel like. Carol was an equal-opportunity insulter. "I think I know what I'm doing."

"I know Marion & Co.," he countered. "This is relationship selling at its toughest. You can't just—"

"I've got it handled, Mark," she said, and then turned back to her laptop.

Mark squinted. At least she'd momentarily distracted him from thoughts of Sophie—but he was starting to get a sinking feeling of despair, and while it was different from mind-bending infatuation or soul-grinding lust, it wasn't a great replacement. "Don't say I didn't warn you," he said grimly.

She glared at him.

"Is this where the...oh, of course, it must be. Okay, Sophie, here's the room."

On hearing Sophie's name, Mark's head snapped toward the doorway, every nerve standing at attention. He forced himself to breathe deeply, trying to make sure his unruly body stayed in line. He stood when three women entered the room—Sophie trailing behind with her laptop case. With her hair pulled back in a loose braid, wearing a slate-blue dress suit, she looked downright edible.

He felt his heart rate—and other things—start to rise, and quickly shifted his attention elsewhere before things got embarrassing.

He forced himself to examine the other two. One was a younger woman, slightly taller than Sophie, with the same gently curling hair, only a dark honey-blond instead of the toffee-brown he was used to. Her face was less intense, as well...softer. That would have to be the sister. The third woman was obviously Sophie's mother Olivia, the chemist and product developer. She was intense, like Sophie, and obviously older, her hair cut short, almost the same blond shade as the sister's. She looked immaculately made up, but her face and her body language communicated tension, almost to the point of brittleness. She kept whispering sharply to Sophie, who kept whispering back in reassuring tones.

Sophie didn't look his way, he noticed as the Diva Nation party settled into their side of the conference table. She seemed more intent on setting up her laptop than checking out her competition. He should probably do the same, he thought, but like a moth to a candle, he couldn't seem to pull away.

Mrs. Marion came in, looking like a queen, or at the very least a duchess. She was wearing a St. John knit suit—Mark could remember the models who'd worn that sort of thing, from when he worked the runway. It was impossible not to look regal when wearing one, and she was going for very classy intimidation.

This is going to get ugly.

"I'm so excited to see what you both have come up with," she said, her voice rounded and cultured, even as her eyes sparkled with avaricious delight. "I know it's a bit unorthodox to have you both here at the same time, but I think it's better when everyone knows what they're up against. Competition only brings out the best, it's what makes our country work."

Mark struggled not to roll his eyes. He glanced at Sophie, who had a similar look on her face. Of course, she chose that moment to look over at him. They shared a millisecond of mutual amusement, and then both quickly looked away, before anything more heated could be exchanged. Mrs. Marion continued talking.

"Trimera, you appear to be already set up," she said, "so I'll forgo the coin toss, and have you start. Is that all right?"

"Splendid," Carol purred, standing. She quickly distributed the hard copy of her presentation—a sheaf of papers, housed in its own binder.

"All this?" Mrs. Marion said in condescending amusement.

Carol blanched. "I think it will answer the most important questions you might have, Mrs. Marion. We pride ourselves on being thorough."

"Obviously," Mrs. Marion observed wryly. "Very well. You'll have twenty minutes."

Carol went pale. Rather, she went paler. "I didn't think it would be so closely timed," she said, hastily shuffling through her presentation.

"I didn't realize you were presenting a doctoral thesis," Mrs. Marion responded.

For a split second, Mark almost felt sorry for Carol. Almost.

"All right," Carol said. "Trimera has been in business for the past fifty years…."

It was going poorly. Mark could tell that in the first five minutes. What was more, he could tell that Sophie knew. Her sister and mother might not get it, but there was a ghost of a smile haunting the corners of her lips (*those lips, don't think about those lips,* he counseled himself). She was amused, and her eyes were bright and shrewd.

He grimaced. This was a nightmare. For the first time, it occurred to him that the promotion he'd been bucking for was in jeopardy. He'd promised Sophie that her business would not be affected if they slept together.

What he hadn't realized was *his* business would be affected. He should have been more on top of this account, and not so intent on sexually pursuing his competitor.

Not just your competitor. Sophie. *There is a difference.*

But different or not, he wouldn't be able to keep Sophie, she'd made that clear. And if he didn't get the promotion—if they kept thinking of him as merely a pretty-faced deal-closer…

Aw, hell.

"You're not really answering my questions. In fact, I can't imagine what questions you are answering," Mrs. Marion finally cut in impatiently, after seeing the thirtieth slide. "What, exactly, is Trimera coming up with for our house brand? What's the ruling concept?"

Carol stammered. "The point is, Trimera products have already done historically well at Marion & Co.," she said, sounding less and less sure of herself. "With our product designers and graphic designers, we can come up with whatever you'd like and make it highly profitable." She quickly switched to a slide of three mock-ups of cosmetics. They were unimpressive. One even said House Brand on it. Mark felt acutely embarrassed and glared at Carol.

"I see," Mrs. Marion mused. "So, what you're saying is…you'll develop whatever we come up with? Whatever possible concept we could imagine?"

"Exactly," Carol said with obvious relief. She even shot Mark a smug grin.

"So why, exactly, would we be paying you when we're doing the hard part?"

Carol blinked, blindsided. "I'm sorry?"

"I don't need a manufacturer, and I don't need a brand name," Mrs. Marion responded sharply. "I need a specially designed product line. This is not what I had in mind. Do you have any suggestions at all?"

Carol was now officially aghast…and to his surprise, she turned to Mark. "Uh…"

He stood up. "Marion & Co. has a long history in quality, high-end retail. If you're offering a line of cosmetics, we would suggest something that reflects not only quality, but classic beauty, with overtones of pampering. What we'd suggest is a luxury line of cosmetics—nothing trendy or over-the-top. Indulgences, aimed for the high-end cosmetics client. I would even recommend calling it Indulgences," he added, spur of the moment.

Mrs. Marion smiled again. "I see. And you don't think that would be boring?"

Mark smiled back, his very best persuasive smile.

"Nothing's more beautiful than classic elegance, Mrs. Marion."

To his delight, she actually beamed back at him. He figured that would resonate, considering how she dressed, how she acted—how she obviously pictured herself, the ultimate Marion & Co. client.

"Well, that's one way to go," Carol said, seemingly more confident. "Beyond that, if you'll look at the proposal, you'll see that—"

"I'll look over the details of your proposal in this very comprehensive pack tonight," Mrs. Marion promised. "At my leisure."

And just like that, Trimera's portion of the program was done. Carol looked a bit shell shocked as she shut off her projector and sat down next to Mark. She glanced at him briefly, her expression clear: *What the hell happened here?*

She couldn't say he didn't warn her, Mark thought. Still, it was a bad start. He wondered how Sophie would do.

Sophie quickly distributed a very neat, very small-looking portfolio to Mrs. Marion's hands. She smiled at Carol and him, quietly confident. It was sexier than hell.

When isn't the woman sexy?

"I agree with Trimera," Sophie said, surprising him. "There's nothing more beautiful than classic elegance. And it certainly doesn't have to be boring, because beauty is more than surface details. We at Diva Nation feel that beauty is an attitude…something that we feel we've captured in the concept for Marion & Co."

Smart girl, Mark thought admiringly. Using Trimera's last and possibly only useful concept, and twisting it to fit what they had.

She was, he realized, about to kick his ass.

She clicked on her presentation, and there was a fully developed, sharp-looking product line, full of bold colors and whimsical yet elegant packaging. "We call it the Screen Goddess line," Sophie said.

"Very interesting," Mrs. Marion said, and there was nothing smug or baiting about it, unlike her interactions with Carol. "It's not too retro, is it? I mean, it wouldn't be old? You've got Greta Garbo, Betty Grable, Veronica Lake…"

"Marilyn Monroe, Catherine Deneuve, Audrey Hepburn," Sophie continued. "I think it's just retro enough. If you consider the fact that you're partnering with Diva Nation—that is, if you decided to partner with us," she said, smiling cheekily at Mark and Carol, "you'll already have a built-in element of urban cool. This way, you're not alienating your older client base, and you're also drawing in a younger demographic."

"Fascinating," Mrs. Marion said. "So we win, all the way around."

It was brilliant, Mark thought. Sophie and Diva Nation had correctly read Marion & Co., developed a perfect, bite-sized presentation, and had subsequently blown Trimera out of the water.

"Well, you two have definitely given me a lot to

think about," Mrs. Marion said, although she barely looked at the Trimera side of the room. "Lily will send you the parameters for the next meeting. You've shown me concepts—now, I want you to show me products. Good luck."

With that, they were dismissed. He saw Sophie high-five her sister before whispering, again, with her mother. They were all triumphant. But before they could leave entirely, Sophie shot him a look that he couldn't quite place. He kept thinking of it after she left, and as Carol picked up the pieces of her crumbled presentation.

Now, he suddenly got why he couldn't quite place Sophie's last gaze. Normally, it was one of either nervousness or pure desire.

This was one of apology…and possibly pity.

Grimly, he set his jaw. She'd been right. Sex between the two of them could be disastrous.

For him.

"We did it! We did it!"

Sophie smiled weakly. Her mother and sister were doing victory dances in their hotel room, which was definitely hampering their attempts at packing to leave.

"What's the matter, Sophie?" her mother finally said, frowning. "You're certainly not acting like we've aced one of the biggest meetings of our lives."

"We haven't won anything yet," Sophie said cautiously.

Lydia made a raspberry sound at her. "Buzzkill," she accused. "We kicked ass and you know it."

Sophie felt a reluctant grin creep across her face. "We did pretty good," she acknowledged.

"Pretty good? Ha! We made those guys *squirm!*" Lydia trumpeted.

Sophie winced. She shouldn't feel badly. After all, it wasn't as if she had done anything unethical. They had beaten Trimera soundly, and on good solid principles.

Still, it hadn't felt good to watch Mark get trounced.

He would be the first to tell you that it was just business, Sophie.

She took a deep breath. Of course, he had told her that after they'd made long, languorous love, back in a hotel room in San Francisco…and he'd assured her that they could keep their emotions separate from their logical, professional lives. It had been almost a month since she'd seen him again, and she hadn't even spoken to him in the interim. She'd indulged in a few brief text messages, saying she was thinking about him. He'd sent back slightly more graphic texts, ones that had stirred her up even as she smiled, thinking about them.

And now, their first face-to-face had resulted in her whipping his company—beating him. She wondered if he still had the same stance.

"Honey, you really need to learn to loosen up," her mother said in her singsong voice. "You'd think we lost, with that look on your face. What's bothering you?"

Sophie tried to school her expression to something less worried. "I was thinking about what we've got ahead of us."

"Oh," her mother said, her expression also reflecting concern. "Are we in trouble, then? I thought we'd done really well." She wrung her hands, sending Lydia a quick look. "I thought—you know—the company was going to be fine."

Lydia made a dismissive gesture, grimacing at Sophie. "You're always focusing on the negative, sis," Lydia said. "I know this thing's a big vendetta for you, a way of sticking it to big companies like Trimera for what they've done to people like Mom. But you've got to learn to savor your victories. Smell the roses. Stuff like that."

"Whatever." Sophie tried not to roll her eyes.

"Don't do that," Lydia warned. "I know you. You're thinking, Lydia went to art school, she's too granola-hippie-flower-child, but I know what I'm talking about here. You're going to burn out if you don't take a break."

"This stuff is too important to the company," Sophie said around a sigh. "I'll take a break when it's all over."

"There are more important things in life than business," Lydia intoned, and it reminded Sophie of her phone conversation with Mark, who had said something similar.

"I know," Sophie said. "I just… It's hard for me to turn my back on it."

"Nobody's telling you to abandon Diva Nation," Lydia said, her voice more gentle. "But you're no good to any of us if you snap and flip out before the deal's done."

Sophie took that silently. For all her "flower-child" ways, Lydia could be very pragmatic.

"You need to find some sort of stress relief," her mother said. "You need a hobby."

Sophie laughed. "What, like macaroni art?"

"No, wait, Mom's onto something," Lydia agreed. "You definitely need to figure out a way to replenish. Mom's going to be doing the heavy lifting for the next round, anyway. I'll do packaging, Mom will do product. You should do something to take the edge off in the meantime."

"We can talk about it when we get home," Sophie said, feeling weary right down to her toes. On the flight back to L.A., she wanted to go over the numbers Carol had been spouting off about Trimera. Carol might have misread Marion & Co., but Sophie could use that information nonetheless….

To Sophie's surprise, her mother shook her head, taking her suitcase out of her hand. "Your sister and I have decided," she said firmly, "that you need a vacation. You should stay here in Vegas for the weekend."

"Here?" Sophie said, grimacing. "Why? I don't even gamble."

"The hotel has a great spa," Lydia said as she finished packing her own suitcase. "There's art galleries, there are shows, there's a ton of stuff to do. Mom and I will get to work, but you definitely need a break. So don't show up at the office until after this weekend." Lydia scooped up Sophie's laptop.

"Hey!" Sophie made a grab for it, but her mother prevented her, shaking her head.

"Your sister's right. You're working too hard," her mother said. "So take this weekend off. We love you."

They both hugged her, then took their luggage and left.

Sophie sat in the hotel room, looking around, feeling restlessness jittering across her skin. Without her laptop, she had nothing to do. She still had the adrenaline from the presentation pumping through her system, but no outlet for it.

I wonder where Mark is?

She felt a flush of excitement start to curl through her, starting with her stomach and radiating out to her breasts and between her legs. Now that the excitement and stress of the presentation had passed, she felt almost dizzy with relief.

If he meant what he said, she thought, stroking her fingertips over her cell phone, *then he's absolutely right. Being "involved" didn't affect our business one bit.*

The more she thought about it, the more liberating the idea became. She had thought that sleeping with Mark would be one of the most disastrous acts in her life—personally damaging, as well as professionally, since her business and personal life were so inexorably intertwined. But she'd had an incredible night with him, and then she'd managed to pull off one of the biggest successes in Diva Nation's history.

She grinned broadly. She was worrying about nothing. And she really *did* need to relax, and get rid of some stress.

I know the perfect hobby.

She called up Mark's cell phone. It rang several

times, then shifted over to his voice mail. "I can't answer the phone right now," his voice said, the drawl eliciting another shiver through her. "Please leave a message."

"Mark," she said after the prompt, her own voice going husky. "I'm staying in Vegas through the weekend. I was wondering, do you think you'd be free? I don't know what your plans are, but I'd love to spend some time together."

She left it at that, hanging up. She hadn't packed anything sexy, so she decided to go down to the hotel shop. It was Vegas, she reasoned. There had to be a lingerie shop somewhere in Sin City.

She smiled. Mark might make the perfect hobby, after all.

THAT NIGHT, MARK STAYED UP in his room at the hotel, refusing Carol's halfhearted dinner invitation. The two of them had already said all that needed to be said after the presentation itself.

"Well, that went swimmingly," he'd said, as Carol had packed up her laptop disconsolately. He didn't want to tell Carol *I told you so.* No—he *did* want to tell her that, but knew it wasn't the productive thing to do. He'd watched as Sophie and her family had left, obviously ecstatic. He couldn't quite sort out his own feelings at that point. All he knew was Trimera had lost. Not just lost—they'd made fools of themselves.

If only I'd pushed Carol harder, he thought frantically. *If only…*

There were too many "if only" statements that could be made. None of them were productive either.

If only I had been able to get my mind off of Sophie Jones...

He sighed. That was the least productive of all.

"Mark, we need to talk."

This, from Carol. Mark had grimaced, then had decided to put his best "we can work it out" face on. "Sure," he'd said easily. "We didn't do as well as we'd hoped—" and if that wasn't an understatement, he didn't know what was "—but I still think we can pull it out for next time. In fact, I have a few ideas—"

"You know," Carol had interrupted him, a pensive look on her face, "I've decided that you were right. About everything."

Her abrupt about-face caused him to goggle with surprise. He got his composure back a moment later. "I'm right about what?"

"You should have been point person on this product proposal," she said with a decisive nod. "In fact, I'm going to go back to my room and call Roger and Simone right now."

"Uh...thanks," he said finally. Carol was a pit bull— seeing her give this up was like watching a starving fight dog walk away from a sirloin steak. Although, she wasn't known for her altruism, either. "Why the sudden change of heart?" he added carefully.

She shrugged. "It's obvious that you know the client," she said simply. "You even know the competition."

He wasn't sure if there was a dig in that last remark, but for the most part, he gathered that the whole thing was a compliment. She was finally acknowledging he was more than a pretty face—someone to charm female distributors out of lots of sales. He was more than fancy packaging. His chest swelled with pride, but he kept his tone modest. "Thanks, again. I appreciate it." He frowned. "I get the feeling Roger might not share your enthusiasm, though." But now that he'd won Carol over, things might be starting to head his way.

"Not to worry, I'll handle that," Carol assured him. "I'm sure you can handle the next meeting, the San Francisco one, by yourself. Besides, I've got a ton of other work that I should have focused my attention on, anyway."

He felt the slightest chill of apprehension. This was more than making him point person. It sounded as if she was stepping out entirely. "Well, your work has been very valuable…."

"And I'll send out an e-mail to everyone," she said, snapping her laptop shut and zipping it into its case with a loud flourish of finality, "letting them know that from now on, Marion & Co. is your baby. Everything will be in your hands from now on. This is your project—run with it."

That was when it hit him, and he went cold.

She wasn't acknowledging his intelligence, his strategy or his skills. She had already determined that this account was a loser, which would piss off the powers-that-be something fierce—and she was distancing herself from it as fast as possible. What was more, she was putting *him* in front of it, so when it failed, all people would remember was "it was Mark McMann's baby, and he flubbed it."

His momma had raised him better than to call a woman names, but he still thought some vile adjectives about Carol, even as he smiled politely. "Thanks," he repeated, keeping his voice light.

She returned the smile, probably thinking he was too dumb to figure out what she'd just done to him. "Absolutely no problem."

So now he was in his room, desperately trying not only to salvage the hope of a promotion, but to save his own ass.

There was a knock on his door, and he frowned. Had he ordered room service? He'd meant to, twice, but he'd gotten sidetracked by Internet research—trying to figure out Trimera's next plan of attack. Now, he couldn't remember if he'd made a call downstairs or not. He got up, wincing at the stiffness of his legs from sitting at the small desk for several hours, and then opened the door.

Sophie was standing there. She was still wearing the same suit she'd been wearing at the Marion & Co. presentation, looking a little tired and rumpled, but otherwise looking the same as always.

In other words, tempting.

He took a deep breath. "You shouldn't be here," he forced himself to say.

She was glancing up and down the hallway. "I wanted to talk to you," she said. "Can I come in?"

He knew he shouldn't. Hadn't he already determined that she was part of the problem? But at the same time, he wanted to hear what she had to say—and he couldn't very well have a conversation out there, in the hallway. They'd be spotted for sure, by somebody in the industry. This was a fairly large convention, after all.

"All right," he said. *But just for a minute,* he assured himself.

Even if he didn't believe it.

He closed the door behind her, and she turned. Before he realized what she was up to, she had looped her arms around his neck, getting up on her tiptoes and kissing him tenderly. His first reaction was surprise—he'd always been the aggressor, up to this point. She'd always been the reticent one, the careful one.

What's going on here?

But after that thought, he felt most rational thinking slip away as he reveled in the taste of her, the feel of her heated, compact body against his. He clutched at her hips, pulling her closer to him, and she made a soft moan of contentment.

They finally broke apart, their breathing ragged. "I've been missing that," Sophie admitted in a soft voice.

So had he, he realized. Then rationality set back in. "Where's the rest of your family?"

"They're flying home to L.A. today," she said. "I decided to stay behind for another night."

"Oh?" He tamped down the immediate thought: *She's*

here by herself for the night. She can spend the night with you. "Did you have other work to do? Meetings?"

"Nope," she said, her fingertips stroking over the planes of his chest, the ticklish sensation torturing him beneath his French shirt. "I thought I just needed a break. And I thought you might need one, too."

"You're not usually…like this," he said.

She blushed, and she was more like the Sophie he remembered. "Is it bothering you?"

"No. Not exactly," he amended.

"Do you…" She paused, then cleared her throat. "I thought we were on the same page." She looked at him, her indigo eyes wide and vulnerable. "Don't you want me?"

He sighed roughly. "Of course I want you," he said. "Sometimes I think I can't remember what it was like to not want you."

She leaned against him, her head tucked against his chest, under his chin. "I know how you feel."

"But we said it would be for one night," he said.

"We've said that before," she teased, with a shaky voice. "I figured…"

"One more time wouldn't hurt?" Mark forced himself to take a crucial step away from her, even though his body was now throbbing with need. Just the smell of her perfume was enough to trigger his desire. "Sophie, things have changed."

She stared at him, then frowned. "Why? Because Trimera didn't do well today?"

"Didn't do well. That's putting it mildly," he said, more sharply than he'd intended. "We tanked. You guys ran off with that presentation like we handed it to you on a platter."

"That's not my fault," Sophie protested. "I thought you said that what we do—together—didn't have anything to do with the business, or the competition!"

"I didn't think it did," he said, crossing his arms.

"But now," she said, studying his face intently, "you do."

He let out a frustrated exhalation. "I don't know."

"That's not fair, Mark," she said, her voice low and angry. "You're the one who set the terms of this. I thought it was about…enjoyment. We enjoy each other. *That's it.*"

"So you're here because you were looking for some fun?" he said, his voice caustic.

Her eyes rounded in surprise. "I'm here because I want you."

"I've always had to persuade you," he said. "I've felt *guilty* because I thought I was putting you in an uncomfortable position!"

"But it didn't stop you," she pointed out, and guilt hit him again like a hatchet.

He plowed forward. "Well, it's stopping me now."

"No, it isn't," she said, her voice as sharp as his was. "You think that sleeping with me is somehow jeopardizing your chances at winning this. That's why you're not pressing me, saying we can 'keep it separate.' You don't even believe it anymore!"

"And you do?" he said, feeling angry—and feeling even more guilty, since that was exactly how he was feeling. "Why are you really here, Sophie?"

"Well, it's definitely not to ruin your chances at the Marion account!" Her eyes blazed. "I came here because I wanted you. Because when I'm with you, I feel better than I can remember feeling in months. Hell, *years*. Because you're tender, and amazing, and I have never wanted anybody like this."

Remorse clawed at him. He'd felt that way, too. He still felt that way.

"But there are bigger things than sex involved right now." He couldn't believe he was taking the stance, but there it was.

"This isn't just sex," she said. "I would never put my family's well-being at risk for just *sex*." Her voice was dismissive, making it sound as if he should have known that.

As if he were *stupid*.

He felt his temper, simmering, burst into a full boil. "So what are you putting your family's business at risk for? Why is this so important to you? This isn't even a relationship. I don't know *what* this is!"

She winced, and he only briefly felt a pang, but his temper was a runaway train and there was no stopping it. "You like sex, specifically with me. You're willing to put up with a clandestine affair with me as long as nobody finds out."

"You *know* why nobody can find out!"

"Would you be willing to wait for me?" Mark snapped.

"You want me. This Marion & Co. crap isn't going to last forever. Can you just put it on pause for a few months?"

"You *couldn't!*" Her hands balled into fists. "You *didn't!* I can't believe you're putting me on the defensive because I'm doing what you were doing!"

"What I was doing," he said, "was giving in to lust. What you're doing is using me to blow off steam."

All color drained out of her face.

"You don't want anything more from me than a lay," he said, needlessly cruel. He didn't know why he said it. Maybe because he'd been in this position before. Maybe... "You haven't said you want anything more permanent than that. I figure, you either like the challenge—the forbidden-fruit thing. Or, like you said when we first met—you hadn't had sex in a long time, and work was your life. So I'm just *convenient.*"

"Nothing about you is convenient," she spat out. "And at the moment, I don't want you at all."

He still wanted her—that was the damnable thing. But he had to focus. They didn't have a relationship. She wasn't spouting her undying love, and even if she did, what could they do about it? All she'd admitted to was they were having an affair. He wasn't about to live his life for that. He was worthwhile, damn it. He was intelligent, hardworking, a good guy.

He deserved more than this.

"I think you should leave," he said.

"I'm going," she said, her expression dark. She

paused as his hand rested on the doorknob. "Don't talk to me again. We're going to *destroy* you guys."

He didn't even dignify it with a response. He just let her out into the hallway and shut the door behind her.

He went to the minifridge, pulling out a few of the tiny bottles: vodka, whiskey, scotch. He then proceeded to open and drain each one.

Damn her. He hadn't even meant those things, had he?

Why couldn't he *think* when it came to Sophie?

And what was he going to do now?

5

"HOW'S THE WORK COMING?" Sophie's mother said, peeking her head into the living room.

Sophie gritted her teeth, her grip on her wooden pencil as tight as an iron vise. "Mom…"

Her mother frowned. "I waited a whole hour before I asked."

"You're not helping," Sophie said in a low voice. "It's fine. I'm doing everything I can. Please keep working on those prototypes, okay? And tell Lydia I want to talk to her about the packaging mock-ups."

"You don't have to be so cranky about the whole thing," her mother responded in a sulky voice.

Sophie sighed, rubbing both hands over her face. Her mother really hadn't done anything to deserve Sophie's ire; Sophie certainly did not have cause to be acting the way she was. The "rejuvenating" weekend her mother had suggested she take had gone completely to hell, thanks to her confrontation with Mark. She'd thrown herself at him.

He'd tossed her back, roughly.

What you're doing is using me to blow off steam. You don't want anything more from me than a lay.

The comments still haunted her—probably because of the element of truth in them.

She wanted more from him than sex, she thought. Admittedly, they couldn't have anything more than sex. Not with the things they wanted, which happened to be in direct competition with each other. She knew it had been crazy, to think they could keep their business and personal lives separate. But he'd felt so damned *good*...

And it hadn't just been the sex. When he'd called her on the phone, she'd felt as if they were truly getting to know each other. If it hadn't been for the Marion & Co. nonsense... If it weren't for the fact that he worked for her mother's sworn enemy, a big conglomerate that was huge and soulless and the same as all the other corporations Sophie had ever worked for...

If only. Sophie huffed, mocking herself mentally. Her life was plagued with vague potentials, bright "what-might-have-beens," and some harsh realities.

Lydia walked in, carrying some cardboard boxes and plastic containers in a small basket. "Here are those mock-ups," she said, tossing the basket on the coffee table next to Sophie's laptop. She sounded snarky, too. Apparently there was something in the water.

Sophie picked up the first box. "I thought we decided on royal-purple, midnight-blue, with silver lettering. Why is this gold?"

Lydia made a face. "Silver is too old. Gold looks better—classier."

"Screen goddesses, remember?" Sophie said. "Silver screen."

"Silver hair," Lydia countered. "Damn it, why don't you let me do what I do? I'm the designer. You're not."

Sophie bit her lip. Why was everyone snapping at her lately? "What the hell is your problem, Lydia?" she asked in a quiet voice. "Because I'm really close to the edge, and I don't need this right now."

"None of us needs it," Lydia snapped. "You're not the only one under pressure!"

This again. If Lydia kept pushing that point, they wouldn't get anywhere. Sophie couldn't fix the thing with Mark—that was a wash, a devastating disaster that had gone past the point of no return. But she couldn't afford to have her sister hating her, too. Especially not when her sister was also the head graphic designer for their family company and a key part of their future success.

"Come on," Sophie said, rising from the couch. "We're getting a coffee."

Lydia looked mutinous for a moment, then nodded. Sophie drove them to the local coffee shop, ordering the two of them some frothy, chocolate-and-caramel latte drinks with plenty of whipped cream. She was gratified to see Lydia smile when she carried the drinks over.

"I figure we could use the rush," Sophie said, putting Lydia's drink in front of her and settling down at the table. "So why don't you tell me what's wrong? I've never seen you like this. Normally you define unflappable. Lately…"

"I know. Lately, it's been like PMS four weeks a

month," Lydia admitted, using a finger to scoop up some of the whipped cream. "I just wish this wasn't so damned important. I feel like our whole life is on the line every time I go to the office."

Sophie sighed. "Yeah. I know that one."

"And it doesn't help that Mom looks at you as the be-all, end-all," Lydia said. "She means well, but she treats me like a flunky, Sophie. It's like I'm not smart enough, or something. I'm barely good enough to be your helper, and I have to take all my cues from you." Lydia's expression of unhappiness tore at Sophie's heart. "I know you guys might not see it, but I'm a damned fine graphic designer. Even though I haven't been out of school for very long, I could be making a good living if I weren't so committed to helping Mom out."

"I believe it," Sophie said.

"But Mom doesn't." Lydia took a long sip of her coffee. "She thinks I'm merely along for the ride. Do you know how hard it is, to always keep proving yourself—and to always come up short?"

"She doesn't mean it," Sophie defended. "You know what she's like. She's right-brained. Scientific."

"Yeah, I do," Lydia said. "I also know that it's an excuse. But lately, she's gotten so focused on the business and being successful and getting revenge on Trimera, she doesn't take time to notice what it actually *does* to the people around her."

Sophie grimaced, taking a long sip of her sugary drink to hide her expression of chagrin. Was that what had happened, with her and Mark? Was she so intent on the business side that she'd deliberately chosen to ignore any possibility of a relationship?

Was that what he was so upset about?

"You're getting that way, too," Lydia pointed out. "I know how hard you've been working on all of this."

"Thanks," Sophie said. "It's not easy."

"Yeah, but you realize you're making it even harder, don't you?" Lydia rolled her eyes. "You're making this a life-or-death struggle. You're making everything much more meaningful and complicated than it needs to be."

Sophie blinked. "It's not only about the business," she protested. "It's like you said. I'm committed to the family. I mean, we can't let Mom flounder, can we?"

Lydia looked contemplative. "I'm not saying we leave Mom to fend for herself," she replied. "But…this is going beyond helping Mom, or being committed to the family company. You're in this for revenge. And you're in this to prove something."

Sophie didn't know what to say to that.

"I've let Mom down tons," Lydia said with a wan smile. "So it's not as hard on me. But you've always been perfect. So it's harder on you. It probably never even occurred to you to tell Mom, 'This is making me crazy. I can only do so much, and at the end of the day, I'll have done the best I can and we'll all have to be okay with that.' Would you say that?"

Sophie winced. "Probably not."

"I rest my case." Lydia took a long last sip of her drink,

sighing with happiness. "Thanks for this. Not just the sugar and caffeine—although they help—but for talking to me." She looked at Sophie with some regret. "I was ready to tell Mom, and you, that I was going to walk."

Sophie cringed. "I'm glad you changed your mind."

"It takes talking. It's more than getting the work done—it's about building understanding," Lydia said, more sage than her twenty-eight years would've suggested. "Mom gets so into the science, and you get so into the business, that sometimes you forget what it's really about."

"Which would be…?" Sophie prompted.

Lydia rolled her eyes. "People," she answered, as if it were patently obvious. Which, actually, it was, now that Sophie thought about it. "Trimera screwed up by not paying attention to the people portion of the program. They thought it was all numbers. You got it." She nodded. "Just don't forget that there are other people than clients and customers, okay?"

Sophie nodded, chastised. She thought about Lydia's remark, all the way home.

She and Mark had talked, but it had never been about anything that involved the two of them. They'd covered superficial stuff, their likes and dislikes, their quirks. They'd gone a bit deeper and talked about their dreams. Sophie had always wanted to work for herself, maybe as a marketing consultant. Mark had revealed his past as a model—something that had not surprised her—and then had revealed that he'd always wanted to make it to vice president of marketing. He wanted to show people that he was more than a pretty face.

She'd never made the connection before, that his business goal and their "personal" relationship might intersect. He'd always made sure that she knew that he didn't want her to feel cheap, or used. He cared about her as a person.

She had not taken the same care. She'd gone to him, assumed he'd be reassuring as usual, and then he'd make love to her as he always had. She'd treated him badly—just a pretty face, or a hunky body, a tool. Not a person, with a brain…and more importantly, a heart. He'd then reacted even worse…and then the two of them had stupidly let the whole thing escalate.

She had to apologize to him. She had to make this right.

She walked into her mother's house, with Lydia humming contentedly as she went back to her room/office to work on new mock-ups. Her mother walked in as Sophie was cleaning off the coffee table. "You're not leaving, are you?" her mother asked, aghast.

Sophie frowned, her hands full of papers. "Well, yeah," she said slowly. "I thought I'd do some more work from my apartment."

And call Mark, she added mentally. Once she figured out what she was going to say, and how she'd apologize.

"But…we still have a ton of things to do!"

"Which I can still do from my place, Mom."

"No," her mother said, getting that stubborn tilt to her head that Sophie knew—and also knew she couldn't fight against. "I'm finishing the last of the eye-shadow color palettes tonight, and Lydia will have the packaging ready. I want to see what you've come up with for the presentation, with all this stuff put in."

"Mom, the presentation's two weeks away," Sophie protested.

"They're going to come at us hard," her mother said, and despite the coldness of her tone, Sophie reacted to the fear in her mother's eyes. "You said that yourself. I can't afford to lose this, Sophie!"

Sophie winced. This wasn't just about the vendetta, as Lydia had said. This really was her mother's future.

"All right, Mom," she said. "I'll stay here, we'll go over what I've got tonight, and then I'll work more from home tomorrow."

"Thank you," her mother said, grudgingly. "You know, it's better to do some things face-to-face. It'll calm my mind."

"Okay." She watched as her mother retreated to her garage lab, and then started putting the papers back on the coffee table, intent on finishing the rough presentation in time to show her mother and sister that evening. Her mother just needed some hand-holding. At least she was letting Sophie and Lydia go on their own to San Francisco, to make the presentation. It did show a level of trust, which Sophie appreciated.

She thought about Mark again. She needed to show *him* a level of trust, she realized. And a phone call might not get it done. Knowing him, he probably wouldn't even answer his phone. He was probably neck-deep in battle strategy, thinking of ways to drive her, and Diva Nation, into the ground.

She couldn't blame him, and she wasn't about to stop working hard. But she was still apologizing and would patch things up. It had never been just business between them sex, either. It was something more. Hopefully, when all of this was over, they'd be able to see exactly what that "something more" was.

In the meantime, she'd wait until San Francisco. And then she'd make her move. As her mother often said, some things were better face-to-face.

ANOTHER WEEK, ANOTHER hotel room, Mark thought. At least this one was nice, with a view overlooking San Francisco's Bay Bridge. Marion & Co. had booked it for him, and Abigail Marion definitely had champagne tastes. The room itself was large for one person, with a California king-size bed, a cherry desk with a large work surface, modem port and fax, a flat-screened television and vaulted ceilings. The decor itself was sumptuous, all in shades of dark blue and teal with green accents. Even the minifridge had splits of Cristal and small bottles of Courvoisier. It was very, very luxurious.

Too bad I'm not in any shape to enjoy it.

Mark had come in a day early. Simone was arriving in tomorrow, ostensibly to give moral support—which, loosely interpreted, meant making sure he didn't screw up. He'd been working on the damned presentation eighteen hours a day for the past three weeks. He'd worked while eating. He'd damned near worked while showering. He dreamed about this presentation.

That was, when he wasn't dreaming about Sophie.

He rubbed at his eyes with the heels of his palms. No. He wasn't thinking about Sophie until he absolutely had to, which would be tomorrow at four o'clock, when they faced off again in front of Abigail Marion. When he saw if he had what it took to win the second "challenge."

It would be an uphill battle without question. He hadn't had a lot of help from Trimera. Carol, bitch that she was, had quickly spread around the rumor mill that the reason Trimera had performed poorly in the first challenge was that she'd been handicapped by having Mark as a teammate. Because no one else had been at the presentation, and everyone knew what a sales barracuda she was compared to Mark's easygoing style, they all assumed that she was telling the truth. Now, everyone in sight refused to have anything to do with what they were calling the "Marion Disaster." Mark had fought to get information he needed for his report, and to get mock-ups ready, but he'd gotten static at every turn. He'd kicked butt around the office, something he rarely did in order to get his work done. Of course, in his current snarling state of mind, it hadn't been hard to kick some butt. He wasn't some pretty-boy model who had made it on just his looks—or by screwing his way to the top sales position.

He frowned. Which brought him right back to his problem with Sophie.

He didn't know who he was more mad at: Sophie or himself. She had valid points. It wasn't as if he'd ever promised her a relationship when they'd slept together, images of which were burned indelibly in his memory. It wasn't even as if she were evil for wanting some sex to get rid of stress. He was currently in an insane pressure cooker of stress, and if sex would relieve it, then he would probably do the same thing.

But Sophie was different, damn it.

It was unfair of him to get angry with her. He was trying to make her pay for the fact that almost everyone in his life—from his modeling days, to business school, to Trimera itself—had always looked at him as someone they could use for superficial purposes, not someone who made a valuable contribution. He wanted to feel valued. And with Sophie, he supposed he'd been starting to feel that way. Then he'd lashed out at her, because of the Carol fiasco, because he could see his professional future circling the drain. Because Sophie couldn't seem to see how important everything was to him, and only focused on the physical.

And why shouldn't she? She's not your wife. She's not your girlfriend. She's just somebody you slept with.

There was a knock on his door, and he sighed, thinking about the last time there had been a knock on his hotel-room door. But after the way his last exchange with Sophie had ended, he couldn't imagine she'd be back. He certainly wouldn't be.

He peered out through the peephole.

Sophie stood there, yet again.

He opened the door, feeling numb. He couldn't say anything for a long moment. Her hair was down, tumbling loosely around her shoulders, looking like ribbons of caramel, luscious and rich. Her eyes were luminous. She wasn't wearing much makeup. What she was wearing, he noticed, was an expression of hesitance.

"Hi," he finally said, feeling unsure himself.

"I won't blame you if you don't want to let me in," she said, her voice speeding up a little. "But I hope you will."

He moved away from the door frame, letting her walk past him, and then shut the door behind her, still at a loss for words.

She turned, wringing her hands slightly. "I came to apologize."

Now she'd really caught him flat-footed. "Okay."

"I'm not sorry I wanted to have sex with you," she clarified.

"Uh, that's good." Because at the moment, his body was going into full alert, the way it always did around her. The scent of her tickled his nose, and his body tensed pleasurably.

"I'm sorry that I made it seem like I saw you as a body." Her eyes were sorrowful. "That I was using you."

It was like being splashed with cold water. He turned away from her, getting his bearings. "I should probably say it's fine," he said slowly. "I mean, we didn't have any kind of understanding. Hell, every other time, I was the one convincing you."

"I know," she answered. "I took that for granted. I took *you* for granted." She walked over to him, stroking her hands over his shoulders and back. "I didn't mean to."

"It hurt," he admitted, surprising himself. "I'm used to being underestimated and written off because of the way I look. I just wasn't expecting it from you."

She tugged at him, turning him to face her. "I'm so sorry, Mark," she said simply.

He wanted to resist, but she pulled at him, and it was as futile as fighting the tide. He leaned into her embrace, letting her hug him, feeling the knots of anxiety and pressure start to slowly ease away in the face of her warmth. He clung to her, holding her against him like a lifeline. "You shouldn't have to be sorry," he told her.

"Hush. Let me make it up to you." She smoothed her hands over his chest, around his waist. "How can I help you feel better?"

He chuckled weakly. "Isn't this how we keep getting into trouble?"

"It doesn't have to mean sex," she said. "Sit down for a second."

She nudged him toward the bed, and his body hardened in a rush as it did every time he was near Sophie and a bed. His responses were almost instinctual now, when it came to her.

She stood in front of him, framing his face in her hands. "That presentation—and Marion & Co.'s response to it—wasn't your fault," she said. He blinked, surprised by the turn of the conversation. "That idiot woman didn't know who she was dealing with. I could tell that you didn't agree with what she was doing. And I know you. You're a better businessman than that."

"How can you tell?" He felt like an idiot, but a small part of his heart warmed at her words.

"Because I've talked to you. I've spent time with you," she continued, stroking his cheek. "You're intelligent, you're intuitive, and you're amazing with people. I bet, given the opportunity, you'll be fantastic."

"Of course," he added, his hands reaching for her hips and holding her lightly, "that means being 'fantastic' against you."

"I'm not worried about me," she responded, kissing his jaw. His grip on her hips tightened. "If I can't compete, that's my problem."

"Easy for you to say." He inched his hands up slightly on her rib cage, resting below her breasts. He'd felt the same way, until she'd trounced him at the Vegas competition.

"I mean it," she said. "When it's business, it's business. It has nothing to do with what we have in private. I promise you—we can keep it separate."

He groaned, leaning his head against the crook of her neck and breathing in her sweet perfume, feeling her breasts fill his hands. "Damn it," he said, "it would be so much smarter if we could leave each other alone."

"Shh," she said, pressing him back against the bed. "It's not a matter of smart or stupid. We need each other.

We want each other. And more importantly, we care about each other."

The moment she said the words, he knew they were true. He cradled her against him, kissing her hair, her neck.

"This isn't just physical," she murmured. "That's why I keep coming back."

"Sophie," he breathed.

She reached for his pants, unbuckling them, lowering them down off his body. He reached for her jeans, taking them off, enjoying the lovely view of her. He took off her tank top; she took off his shirt, until they were both naked. She shook her head when he reached for her, though.

"I want to make you feel better," she said, her gaze slightly naughty, but with an undercurrent of seriousness. "This isn't about me."

"But I…*oh.*" He stopped abruptly when she leaned down, pressing heated kisses down his torso, around his belly button. He stopped breathing altogether when she got lower, kissing his thighs, creeping higher. She cupped his balls, and he let out the breath he was holding in an explosive whoosh. "Sophie," he growled.

She took his cock into her mouth, tickling the tip gently, grazing him ever so minutely with her teeth. He grimaced, his hips bucking slightly of their own accord. She started sucking on him, slow, measured draws, flooding his body with sensation. His breathing went harsh and ragged in response. He could feel her tongue dancing over him, sliding around the length of him as she took him in as deep as she could. The wet, heated caress of her mouth pushed him toward the breaking point.

"Sophie," he said, his fingers twining in her hair. "I need you."

She pulled away, and he could see her eyes were bright, her cheeks flushed. "You have me," she said with a small smile. "This is all for you."

He moved quickly, shifting her onto her back. "As great as it feels," he said, kissing her breasts, "it isn't for me unless you're there, too."

He got up, hastily getting a condom and rolling it on. Then he reached for her again, and she arched her hips up to meet him. He slid in, surprised to find how wet she was, simply from pleasuring him. "How did I get lucky enough to find you?" he said.

Then all talking ceased, as he felt her body tighten around him. He moved slowly, savoring each stroke, until she was wild beneath him, her hips pistoning against his, her legs curling around his waist. Despite his best intentions, he found himself picking up speed, as her nails clawed gently down his back. Soon they both were panting, clutching each other, until the pressure built inevitably to its explosive conclusion. He shouted her name as he slammed into her, and she cried out as she clung to him, their bodies so close that they seemed inseparable.

After long moments, he felt his mind return from the blissful release. He rolled to his back, taking her with him, resting her on his body. "I mean it," he said. "I'm so lucky I found you."

"It'll be all right, Mark," she assured him. "I promise. We can do this." And she kissed him, her smile wide and hopeful.

"If you say so," he said, even as worries started to return, too. She said it would be all right. She said she believed in him. She knew he could do well.

Now, all he had to do was actually do the job—and see if she felt the same way in the morning.

6

"WHERE WERE YOU LAST NIGHT?" Lydia whispered to Sophie in the small conference room in the hotel. "I called your room to do some last-minute walk-throughs, but there was no answer. I worried!"

Sophie forced herself not to glance over at Mark. "I was going stir crazy and decided to go out." She grinned. "What are you, my mother?"

"You're lucky I'm not Mom," Lydia muttered back. "I still can't believe you convinced her to stay home for this as it is. But don't change the subject. Where'd you go?"

"I took a walk," Sophie improvised. "Wanted to get my head clear for today, that's all."

Lydia looked unconvinced, but let it drop, thankfully. "I hope it worked. Those guys look mean."

Sophie used the excuse and shot her gaze over to the other side of the room. Mark looked… Well, she wouldn't say *mean*, unless *mean* meant razor-sharp and smokin' hot. He was every inch a professional in an expensive charcoal-gray suit with a royal-blue silk tie over a sparkling white shirt. His face was clean shaven and surprisingly stern. Nothing of the carefree lover she remembered from the previous night remained.

"He looks like he means business," Sophie mused, then winced when Lydia's eyebrows shot up at the comment. "And the, er, other lady. His boss. She looks pretty fierce herself."

Lydia did not look appeased, but before she could remark further, Mrs. Marion and Lily Hunter walked into the room.

"Thank you all for coming." Mrs. Marion sat at the head of the table. She always sounded amused—and not necessarily in a nice way. The habit was starting to make Sophie uncomfortable. "I'm very interested in seeing what you came up with for this next round of presentations. I trust you have everything you need?"

Before Sophie could answer, Mark spoke up, his voice clear and authoritative. "We're ready."

Sophie's eyes widened. She'd never heard him sound like that, either. Usually his drawl was just this side of casual. Now, there was an underlying tension. She knew how much this meant to him. Hadn't she encouraged him last night?

Don't be nervous, she silently counseled. Then she saw that Mrs. Marion was staring at her expectantly. "We're set," she added, but it sounded hesitant compared to Mark's ringing assertion.

"Since Trimera started off at the first presentation, I thought Diva Nation ought to have the first shot this time," Mrs. Marion said, steepling her fingers together and sporting a wry smile. "You'll be starting, Ms. Jones. After your last presentation, I'm looking forward to being impressed."

Sophie smiled back easily. "I certainly hope you will be. We've been working hard on developing a line of cosmetics that I think will impress your most discerning customers."

With that, she launched into her presentation, using Lydia's examples. She was proud of what they'd come up with. The packaging was midnight-blue with silver detailing, just as she'd suggested. The ads they'd mocked up were both classic and modern—hip, without being dated. They then handed Mrs. Marion the cosmetic samples themselves, which Sophie considered their ace in the hole. "As you can see, the cosmetics themselves are of the highest quality material and feel as luxurious as the packaging. Our cosmetics are noted for feeling 'naked'…that is, you won't even be aware of wearing them. They're light, fresh and hypoallergenic."

Mrs. Marion brushed some of the foundation over the back of her hand, sniffing experimentally. "And a nice fragrance, too."

"Another one of our signatures," Sophie said with pride.

"I see you've expanded on the promise you showed in Vegas," she said, and Sophie felt a thrill zip through her system. "This is very, very exciting."

"Thank you. I assure you, it's just the start." With that, she sat down. Lydia reached over and squeezed her hand. Sophie had done well—she'd done her best, and it looked very good for her, her family and Diva Nation.

"All right, Trimera," Mrs. Marion said, turning to Mark and his boss. "I'd hate to follow that act, but you're on."

Mark wore a slight frown, a less intense version of the frown his boss was sporting. For a second, Sophie felt a pang of remorse. She knew how much this presentation meant to him. He was trying to prove himself as a businessman, and this was a big deal. He was used to being considered a pretty face and nothing more…. Used to being the salesman who closed deals simply because female buyers found him attractive. That wasn't going to work here. Still, they were in competition. He knew that. Sophie couldn't feel bad that she'd tried hard—this meant a lot to her, too.

"Diva Nation's products are incredible," he started, surprising her. "They have all the advantages of being a boutique line—unique products, niche marketing, a definite cachet among their clients."

Sophie's eyes widened, and she noticed a similar look of surprise crossing his boss's face. What was he doing? He was helping out his competitor, not pushing his own product!

"What they can't do—and what they won't tell you—is that they have all the same problems of a boutique line," he continued. "They are small enough to have difficulties producing their cosmetics. They can't place orders large enough to get the materials they need in a timely fashion. When they can place large orders, they are used to producing in smaller batches, so there are quality issues that crop up. Their packaging is innovative, but not necessarily able to make the profit margin that you'll want...."

Sophie watched as Mark produced a slide show. In a matter of minutes, he'd illustrated all the problems of working with her company—using information she didn't even know he had. He'd talked to all of their most problematic vendors, and he was dead-on when it came to the flaws in their business. She felt her face redden. She felt as if she were standing in the middle of the conference room in a pair of ratty granny panties with holes in them. She was exposed—and humiliated.

"Trimera may not have the innovation that a small company has," he said, sounding like a lawyer at a hanging trial. "But what we do have is the ability to produce on the scale that Marion & Co. will want, with a price point and profit margin that your company will need. Creativity is important." He glanced over at Sophie, and she swore his look was one of contempt. "But then...so is the bottom line."

Mrs. Marion took the whole thing in, nodding thoughtfully. "So—do you have a product line for me?"

He produced a silver cosmetics box, similar to the type professional makeup artists use. "This is the mock-up," he said. "But you'll be emphasizing high quality and discretion. Like the Tiffany pale blue box signifies quality, the Marion & Co. 'silver box' can become a symbol of high-end makeup.... Its own brand recognition." He glanced at the Diva Nation packaging and example ad, and sneered slightly. "Your customers are discerning enough to know what they want, without a bunch of hype."

And with that, another body slam to Diva Nation. Lydia looked pale. Sophie imagined she didn't look much better.

Mark had done more than his homework. He'd systematically *demolished* Diva Nation with that presentation. And she felt devastated.

"And please keep in mind if any of the cosmetics need improvement," he added quietly, "we can always change formulas—and mimic things that are going on in the market."

Lydia gasped, and Sophie saw red. "You're not suggesting that you could knock off Diva Nation products," she interjected, between gritted teeth.

He shrugged. "Business is business."

"Well, this has been a big day," Mrs. Marion said, before Sophie could growl back a retort—and possibly jump over the conference-room table and strangle Mark. "You two have given me a lot to think over. I'd like to see one final presentation in two weeks in New York, at our office there. I need to see how you both envision your companies working with ours, as it were." She smiled. "Meaning why it would make financial sense for Marion & Co. to work with you, rather than your opponent. Although I must say, Trimera seems to have gotten a jump-start on that today. If you need anything, feel free to contact Lily in the interim."

With that, Mrs. Marion and Lily left, after shaking hands with everyone.

"Oh, my God," Lydia breathed, her voice faltering. "Mom's going to freak out when she hears about this. What are we going to do?"

Sophie didn't say anything. She glared at Mark, who was shaking hands with his boss. That woman had a broad smile on her face, full of satisfaction, like a cat in front of a bowl full of cream. Mark didn't share the look, a small comfort. He still had that stern expression, like a soldier at war.

Then, for a second, he glanced over, his gaze locking with Sophie's. He looked…resigned. Possibly even apologetic. Within seconds, he looked determined again, as he snapped his attention back to his boss and his side of the table.

It's just business, Sophie. She closed her eyes, mocking herself. Certainly she'd said it was just business. She wanted him to feel better about the fact that they were competitors. She knew that he had talent.

She just didn't realize that he would use that talent, intelligence and drive, and focus it on a character assassination of her company.

"What are we going to do?" Lydia repeated, her voice injected with a note of hysteria.

"Calm down," Sophie said in a low, sharp tone. "I'll handle it."

"But how?"

"I don't know," she snapped, causing Lydia to finally

quiet down, looking a little wounded. "I was expecting them to push harder, but I wasn't expecting them to play dirty."

"They wouldn't really knock off our products, would they?" Lydia said.

Sophie continued staring at Mark, watching as he and his boss disappeared out of the conference room. "I wouldn't have thought so," she admitted. "But after today…I expect anything."

"Mom was right," Lydia said. "They're heartless. They'll do anything to win."

Sophie closed her eyes. She didn't want to believe it. Not of Mark.

"Maybe," she forced herself to admit. Then she opened her eyes. She had gotten herself into this mess. Crying about it wasn't going to help her situation any. "It means we'll have to toughen up, that's all."

And it means I'm going to rethink my "relationship" with Mark McMann, she thought, agitated. She wouldn't be his judge and jury. But she still couldn't help but wonder why he'd done what he'd done—and whether or not he was the man she'd thought he was, or if she'd just made a colossal mistake.

"SOPHIE, I NEED TO TALK to you."

Sophie was sitting by herself at a table in the hotel bar when she heard Mark's voice behind her. "I don't think I've got anything left to say to you, Mark." She glanced around. "Besides, we shouldn't even be seen together."

He was still in his suit, and his expression was bleak. "I wanted this to be more private," he murmured. "But you wouldn't return my calls."

"Lydia's upstairs packing, Mark," she said. "She'll be down any minute. And there really isn't anything else to say."

He sat down, and Sophie felt a lash of pain shoot through her. Here he was, his face the picture of concern. But he was the one who had hurt her in the first place. What good was it now that he seemed to be sorry for it?

"I was afraid this was going to happen," he said. "You said when it's business, it's business and we can keep it separate, and I wanted you so badly I ignored my damned common sense and let myself believe it."

"This isn't about business," Sophie corrected.

"Oh, come on."

Sophie felt the blush heat her cheeks, and glared at him. "You're right. It is about business. Specifically, it's about how you chose to do business." She lowered her voice to a hiss. "Is Trimera so bankrupt of ideas and innovation that your idea of a great business move is offering to knock off whatever we come up with?"

"I'm not proud of that," he answered. "But it happens all the time, Sophie. That chocolate-cayenne lip gloss your company's so proud of? Three other cosmetics companies will be coming out with it next year, I promise you. I didn't want to have to go that route, but it's a fact of life."

"I thought you'd be winning by pointing out what you guys do well," she countered stubbornly. "Not by underhandedly attacking our company and stealing our ideas."

"It was just business."

"Yeah, well your business *sucks*."

He sighed with obvious frustration. She took a slug of her vodka tonic, gasping back a cough as she gulped too fast.

"It doesn't have anything to do with me and you," he whispered. "It didn't have to do with last night."

She closed her eyes. "I know that." She took a deep breath. "And I finally understand how incredibly naive and stupid I was, to have thought that our arrangement would work."

"You're not stupid," Mark said, sounding aghast.

"Yes, I am. But it's like you said—I wanted you so badly that I was willing to ignore what was staring me in the face." She opened her eyes, feeling tears sting at the corners of them. She wiped them away hastily with her fingertips. "I know we've said it before, but this time, I really mean it. We can't get together again."

"Ever?" Now he sounded bereft.

She bit her lip. "I don't know."

"I don't want to lose you."

The thought of losing him added to the pain she was already feeling. Her emotions were a maelstrom, dark and chaotic. "I don't want to lose you, either," she admitted. "But I don't know how this can work."

"There's too much at stake for both of us," he said. "But this challenge won't last forever. At least give me the hope that when the damned thing is over, we might have a chance."

"One of us is going to win," she pointed out. "And that means one of us has to lose, Mark. As you said, there's too much at stake. Do you really think that we can overlook that when it's all over?"

He fell silent, and the two of them sat that way. It was all Sophie could do not to reach across the small table and take his hand, trying to either comfort him or gain comfort from his touch.

"If I lose," he said, "I'll still want you."

"I'll always want you." The words popped out, unbidden, and she cursed herself for them.

His eyes lit. "Then there *is* hope."

"I don't know," she repeated. "All I know is, we've got two weeks, and then we'll know what happens, one way or the other. Until then—we've got to leave each other alone, Mark. We can't keep going on this way. I know it was my idea, but now…we've got no choice."

Mark nodded, standing up, and she stood up, too. "You're headed out today?"

"Our flight's this evening," she said. She didn't want him to leave, she admitted. As much as she knew it was smarter to cut all ties with him, the thought of not talking to him, of possibly never feeling his body against hers, was almost terrifying.

"I'm leaving tomorrow morning," he said, and for a stupid, wild second, she thought about changing her flight—staying for one last night.

Do you really think that you can have one more "just one night"? She winced at her own stupidity.

"Well, then," she said, and held out her hand. "I guess we'll see you in New York."

He took her hand, his warm grip sending shivers shooting through her. "Good luck," he said. "And I really mean that, Sophie. I never meant to hurt you."

She felt sadness like a lead weight on her chest. She nodded curtly. "Well, you won't hurt me again," she responded. "We'll be ready for you."

"I have no doubt." But his voice still sounded full of remorse.

Then, slowly, tenderly, he leaned down and kissed her cheek softly. In that second, she felt as if her heart splintered.

Blindly, she turned, pressing a kiss against his lips. Not the usual conflagration of passion that they usually succumbed to. This was quiet, filled with need—and regret.

She broke away, then turned and headed toward the elevator. Back in the room, Lydia had finished packing. "Mom's meeting us at the airport," Lydia said. "I just got off the phone with her. Says she's not surprised that Trimera's 'big idea' was the ability to steal *our* ideas. She said that there's no way we can trust them and the sooner we bury their asses, the better." Lydia grinned. "And you know when Mom swears, she's got to be super angry."

Sophie listened to Lydia's patter absently, as she zipped up her own bag.

"Are you okay?" Lydia finally asked.

Sophie shook her head. "No. I'm not okay."

"Today was bad," Lydia said. "But we'll get even, don't worry. We've got one more chance. And you know Mom. She's even more creative when her back's to a wall. We'll figure out some way to pull this off."

Sophie stared out the window. The problem was, even if Diva Nation came up with some way to win the final challenge, there was no guarantee that she could still have Mark. And if she did lose, she wasn't sure she could forgive Mark for practicing what he considered "just business."

The way she saw it, there was no way on earth that she could come out of this a winner.

And the way she felt—in a very real sense, she had already lost.

7

"WAY TO GO, MARK!"

Mark walked through the hallways of his office building, distracted. "Uh, thanks," he said, nodding to whoever had called out the kudos. He hurried back to his desk. Ever since word of his coup at the San Francisco presentation had gotten out, he'd been getting congratulatory little e-mails and atta-boys from his co-workers. People he hadn't heard a peep from in his entire duration at Trimera were suddenly taking notice of him. *Everybody loves a winner,* he thought, trying to make the observation amused and not bitter. Even Carol had come up to him when he was getting coffee at the kiosk in the lobby of the building.

"I heard about how you pulled it out at the Marion & Co. presentation," she'd said, her face looking as if she'd choked on a lemon.

"It went pretty well," he'd responded, as low-key as possible…even though it *had* been gratifying to hear her concession. If he'd been more petty, he would've rubbed her nose in the fact that she'd abandoned him and set him up, having every expectation that he'd fail.

How do you like me now, huh? Still think the model is too stupid to handle the business?

But even that second of gloating was shadowed by the fact that Sophie was upset with him. Something he felt torn about.

We can keep it separate.

He glanced at his cell phone, turning it over and over in his hand. He'd wanted to call her every day since the San Francisco presentation a week ago. He'd managed to resist to this point.

Simone walked into the office. "So, how does it feel to be Trimera's great white hope?" She sat down in one of his chairs, beaming. "I knew you had it in you, Mark."

"I appreciate the support, Simone," he said, sitting in his own chair. "I wasn't sure how much you believed in me."

"I believed in you," she scoffed. "No matter what else people said, I knew you had the killer instinct. You know what you've got, and you're not afraid to use it to your advantage."

Mark frowned, unnerved by two parts of that statement…the killer instinct, and knowing what he had and "using it." "I'm not sure…"

Before he could finish, Roger, the VP of marketing, knocked on his door. "Got a minute, Mark?"

"Sure." Mark gestured to another chair, then looked at Simone.

"No, this'll only take a sec," Roger said. "And Simone can stay. I wanted to say, officially, that the higher-ups are very impressed with what we hear happened in San Francisco."

Mark couldn't help it. His chest heated with pride, and he sat up straighter. "Thanks, Roger."

"We had our reservations, believe me," Roger said, deflating Mark's sense of accomplishment a little. "We didn't think you could handle an account of this magnitude. But I saw the presentation and the mock-ups you had built…and the time you had to do all of it." Roger laughed. "If you can beat up the production department enough to get that quality in that short a time frame, then you've practically earned a raise right there!"

Mark laughed politely.

"Anyway, I wanted to let you know that we're keeping an eye on you, Mark," Roger said, and Mark wondered if this was real, or if it was more rah-rah crap, designed to make Mark feel better without having any kind of real power behind it. Roger obviously saw Mark's hesitance because he chuckled again. "No bull-shit, Mark. You keep this up, and we'll put you in charge of the new project…and maybe start grooming you for bigger things, huh?"

Mark's eyes widened. "Things on the marketing side?"

"I'll have another director position opening up soon," he said, and Mark noticed that even Simone looked surprised by this announcement. "You show me you can handle Marion & Co., and I imagine you'll be paving the way for a nice promotion."

"Director," Mark said, savoring the sound of it. It was one step below vice president.

"Just land the damned account, before you start ordering new business cards," Roger said, again with his harsh laugh. "Like I said—we're watching you."

With that, Roger left the office, leaving a stunned Simone and Mark in his wake.

Mark took a minute to process Roger's statement...and offer. It was everything he'd ever wanted. Since he'd gotten his MBA, since he'd joined the company, he'd wanted to prove himself. He'd worked long hours, and taken a lot of flack from people who hadn't thought he was up to the task. How many conferences had he flown out to, no matter how small? How many drunken distributors had he smooth-talked, even as he'd avoided their blatant advances? It had been years of uphill battle, but finally, at long frickin' last, it looked as if it was about to pay off.

"Holy crap," Mark finally said. "I guess he started reading my reports, huh?"

Simone shook her head. "He really didn't like you, either. He was mad when you challenged him at that one meeting. I thought he'd bury you, for sure."

"Well, you've been standing up for me since day one," Mark said, grateful for her loyalty.

"I didn't know they were thinking of looking for another director," she replied, looking shell shocked.

It occurred to Mark—Simone was a director. Which meant that, if he got promoted, he'd be at her level. Obviously this wasn't something she was prepared for.

"We'd still be working together," he said, wondering if that helped or not.

"Oh, I'm taken aback at the speed, but I've always said…you're smart, and you just needed a chance."

To his surprise, she stood up and shut the door, looking at him intently. *Oh, lord, now what?* "Uh, Simone…?"

"I have to ask," she said, leaning against his desk. His entire body tensed, and he leaned away from her, rolling his chair back slightly. "Is it true?"

"Is what true?"

"There's a rumor floating around," she said, her voice conspiratorial, "that you slept with the enemy."

He would not have been more shocked if she had simply slapped him. "What? Where did you hear that?"

"Oh, don't worry—I didn't hear it from somebody at Trimera," she said. "And Roger certainly doesn't know, and I'm not spreading it. But word on the street is, you and that Sophie woman got pretty cozy in San Francisco."

Mark felt his body flush with anger and embarrassment. He knew he should issue a quick denial, but found his lips couldn't form the words.

She sat back down in the chair, laughing. "I knew it. I *knew* it! Didn't I tell you she looked interested in you, back at that first conference?"

Mark couldn't remember, so he sat silent, seething. Who had seen them? Who was spreading the rumor? And how far had it gone?

"I knew that you were sharp," she said, and her tone of admiration made him feel dirty.

"Now wait a minute," Mark said sternly. "I didn't sleep with Sophie for any kind of advantage. Damn it, I didn't get any information from her! I didn't do *anything* with her that helped me win that presentation!"

He immediately realized that he'd confirmed the rumor.

"I didn't say you did," she replied innocently, still looking amused. "But you went after Diva Nation like an attack dog in San Francisco. Even if you weren't involved with her, that was a thing of beauty. But knowing that you could actually sleep with her, and *still* manage to pull off the presentation…" Her knowing grin was broad.

Mark was shaken. "It was just business," he justified.

"That's it exactly. You were able to handle your business, no matter what you were doing in your personal life." She shook her head. "Lots of people thought you were superficial—handsome, charming, and not that smart. But not me. I knew that you had plenty of ambition—and the right sort of brilliance to capitalize on what you had. And like I said, you've got the killer instinct. You won't let anything get in your way."

"I've got ethics."

"Of course you do," she demurred. Somehow, that didn't make him feel better. "Still, I'd cool it with Sophie, if I were you. I understand what you're up to, but other people—like Roger—might not."

"He might pull me off the account?" Again, like a punch in the stomach. Not that it mattered, since Sophie was already out of the picture.

"No, Roger won't care how you got the account," she

said. "But if he thinks you slept with somebody to get it, he'll lose his respect for you." She shot him a quick, gimlet grin. "Besides, Roger's boss is a woman and he might start getting scared that you'll sleep with her, and try to get his job."

"That's not funny, Simone," Mark said darkly.

"Oh, relax." Simone was obviously tickled by the whole situation. "I'm just saying, keep it quiet."

"Getting involved with Sophie was never about the business," Mark said. "And I need you to keep it quiet, too."

"Of course," she repeated. "Mum's the word."

With a wink, she left his office. He did not feel comforted. Simone was now worried about her own position in the company. He knew that she'd seen him as a protégé, of sorts...but she'd expected to be promoted because of that, not to see him start to catch up with her. Now that she was armed with the information that he'd slept with Sophie, it was a matter of time before she saw a use for that information.

He rubbed at his temples. Here he was, on the brink of getting everything he'd wanted professionally—and he was seen, and admired, for being a bloodthirsty shark in order to get it. He was already losing Sophie in his pursuit of the account. Now, he felt perilously close to losing his soul, as well.

There has to be a better solution, he thought grimly. *There has to be another way.*

Suddenly, an answer pierced his thoughts.

If someone had told Simone about him and Sophie,

then the news must have filtered back. Did Sophie know? And did she think that he spread the rumor?

He grabbed his cell phone, started to dial her number…then stopped himself. If she didn't know, how much worse would it be if he told her? Would he be helping her? And would she blame him for convincing her all those months ago to sleep with him in the first place?

He sat, paralyzed. His already untenable situation was getting worse by the minute.

I have to figure out some way for us both to come out winners. That way, he could have the promotion, have the respect he'd been working toward all his life—and keep the one woman who meant more to him than anyone he'd ever cared about, ever.

He closed his eyes.

He was good. When it came to business, he was very damned good. But as good as he was, he had absolutely no idea how he was going to pull this off without some kind of miracle.

"I CAN'T BELIEVE THE NERVE those people have," Sophie's mom said, her face grim. "We've got better products is the bottom line. How do they think they can win?"

"Trimera has all the advantages of a big company behind it," Sophie replied, her own tone subdued. "They're going to offer all kinds of concessions that we can't. Price breaks, incentives, the whole nine yards." She sighed, trying to make sure her mother understood. "One of the main reasons we're trying to land this account is to make Diva Nation profitable enough for you to have a solid retirement, Mom. If we tried to match Trimera's incentives, we wouldn't make any money at all."

Her mother looked heartbroken—and angry. "I can't believe this. They got rid of me once, and now they're doing it again!"

"Mom, you're not helping," Sophie pointed out. "If I were them, that's how I'd attack. I wasn't thinking strategically in San Francisco."

"I don't know *what* you were thinking in San Francisco," her mother said, sounding bewildered and hurt. "Honestly, Sophie! To just…just *sit* there and let them do that to us!"

Sophie let the insult slide—mostly because she agreed with her mother. She didn't know what she'd been thinking in San Francisco. And, consequently, she'd allowed herself to get blindsided.

It's not going to happen again.

Lydia walked in. "I tweaked the packaging," she said, showing the small cardboard mock-ups. "Now, they still incorporate our design sense, but they're closer to what Marion & Co. already has, so they've got the corporate branding thing." Lydia grinned humorlessly. "So now we're ripping off Trimera's idea."

Sophie nodded. "Don't worry about them ripping us off. I think I've got some ways to combat that. The bottom line is, in New York, all we'll have is our product and our innovation. We're going to have to push that."

"Don't you worry," her mother said. "We'll show them."

"Sophie, I wanted to go over our closing argument one last time," Lydia said. "We're off to grab a coffee, Mom. Can I get you anything?"

"Do I look like I need caffeine?" her mother said, then stalked back to her laboratory. "You two go on. I know how you are about your coffee breaks."

"I will be glad when all this is over, no matter what happens," Lydia said as they walked to her car. "Because Mom gets more frantic and more desperate every day, have you noticed? It's starting to really worry me."

Sophie nodded, feeling weary right down to her bones. "I'll be glad when it's over, too," she admitted.

Unbidden, Mark's face popped up in her mind.

Just a hope of a chance…

She shook her head, clearing it. She wouldn't think about Mark. She told herself that hourly…sometimes every other minute. And every time she told herself that, it didn't work.

"I was talking to that vendor, and I think we've managed to fix that problem of getting supplies in high quantity, so Trimera can't hit us with it anymore," Lydia said, as they sat down at their usual table at the local coffeehouse. "But when I was talking to her, I heard something sort of weird."

"Oh?" Sophie asked, not actually listening. She sipped at her mocha.

"Yeah." Lydia peered into Sophie's face. "She said you're sleeping with Mark McMann."

Sophie choked. Lydia handed her a napkin and patted her back.

"I take it that's a yes," Lydia said wryly. "Jeez, Sophie. And you make fun of me for not being your consummate professional. Last time I checked, boinking the competition wasn't something they taught in an MBA program."

Sophie gasped for air. "It wasn't like that," she finally sputtered out.

Lydia's eyes rolled. "You can't possibly tell me you've got a good explanation for sleeping with him."

"Well…no." Sophie stared at the table surface. "But it always made sense at the time."

"He is gorgeous…and charming." Lydia looked at her, her face filled with concern. "He seduced you, didn't he?"

"No!" She remembered that first night they'd almost slept together—how he'd persuaded her, working against her better judgment. "Not exactly."

"Riiiight," Lydia drawled, obviously unconvinced.

"I even seduced him," Sophie added, trying to be fair. "I made the decision, every time. It was my idea."

"Con artists always make you think it was your idea," Lydia said sternly. "Good grief. You're the one who always tells me that Trimera can't be trusted and that big-business types will do whatever they have to, to win. Didn't you think about that when you decided to sleep with him?"

"He didn't use me," Sophie defended. "And before

you go there—I never, ever told him anything about Diva Nation. It was never about the competition."

"How could you think it wouldn't get mixed up in it?" Lydia's voice was edged with exasperation. "I'm a creative type, and even *I* know that one."

Sophie felt her throat close, this time with tears. "Listen, I don't have any excuse for it. It happened."

"You're not the type for casual affairs." Lydia sounded baffled.

"I know," Sophie agreed.

Lydia was silent for a long moment. Then she said, "And this isn't a casual affair, is it?"

Sophie slumped in her chair. "No."

"Are you in love with him?"

"I don't know." As soon as Sophie said it, the truth of the matter seemed to burn in her chest. "Yes. I am in love with him. And I don't know how, or what we're going to do next."

Lydia paused. "I have to hand it to you—you never take the easy road. So, do you think he's in love with you?"

"I don't know. But he cares about me."

"Enough to walk away from this competition?"

Sophie shook her head. "I wouldn't ask him to, Lydia. That wouldn't be fair. I mean, what would you think if he asked that of me?"

"Which brings up my next question—did it ever occur to you to walk away from this competition for him?"

Sophie felt scandalized. "This is too important, Lydia."

"It's business, Sophie," Lydia countered.

"It's Mom's life," Sophie said. "She's counting on us."

"I love Mom, and I've spent most of my life trying to live up to her expectations…and failing miserably," Lydia answered, smirking. "I've worked my hardest for her, but we can't control everything. She's not going to be out on the street, no matter what. I wouldn't let her, and neither would you. So if we don't win this account…she'll be upset, and it'll be harder, but it won't be the end of the world, Sophie."

Sophie shook her head. "That's no way to win."

"Being inflexible is no way to live," Lydia said. "And I'm not saying we should lose just because you fell in love."

"Then what *are* you saying?" Sophie snapped.

Lydia reached over and took her hands. "I'm saying…don't be a butt-head."

Surprised, Sophie actually laughed.

"Mom was burned by love and business—getting fired by Trimera, and having Dad leave us. She's got a lot wrapped up in all this. But just because she's bitter about what happened, and convinced that winning might make everything right, doesn't mean that you have to follow in her footsteps," Lydia explained.

Sophie thought about it. "If we lose, it won't be because I didn't try," Sophie said.

"Nobody's telling you to throw the challenge," Lydia said. "But if we lose…nobody's telling you that you've got to punish the guy because we didn't make it."

"For a kid sister," Sophie said weakly, "you're pretty wise."

"Yeah, well, I'm starting to realize that I was getting sucked up in the need to win," Lydia said. "I love Mom, but sometimes you start to live in her world…where winning is the only option. Trust me, she'll be okay if this doesn't go through. And loving her and wanting to help her doesn't mean that we have to put our whole lives into chaos because she needs us to. That sounds cold, I know."

Sophie sighed. "It's tough, though."

"After this, no matter what, I'm opening my own design consulting company," Lydia said. "I love Mom, but I can't keep working with her. It'll save the relationship for both of us."

Sophie smiled at her, feeling weepy. "I'll help you with your business plan," she offered.

"Thanks, I'll need it." Lydia smiled back. "And after this, no matter what…if you're in love with this guy, I say go for it. Even if it pisses Mom off no end. You're not in high school anymore."

Sophie thought about it. Her mom and the business meant a lot to her—but Lydia was right. It wasn't her life.

"And, we may win," Lydia added, with a wink. "Which brings up the question—will he still love you if he loses to you?"

Sophie closed her eyes. "I'll jump off that bridge when I come to it."

8

MARK SAT IN A CONFERENCE ROOM in Marion & Co.'s New York corporate offices. Simone and Roger were out in the lobby, Simone on her laptop, Roger barking at someone on his cell phone. They had already made their sales pitch to Mrs. Marion, privately—apparently her "open competition" finally had some privacy, probably because she had the instincts of a horse trader: if one company *thought* their opponents were giving a better deal, they'd just keep going lower and lower until Marion & Co. had everything they wanted for a song. He had to admire the woman's shrewdness. After all, it was what had made her family's company such a force to be reckoned with, all these years.

Sophie sat in a corner with her mother and sister. Her mother was shooting poisonous glances in his direction. The sister was more intent on Sophie, who wasn't looking at him at all. They had already had their turn with Marion & Co., as well, and everyone was waiting for the final announcement as far as who'd won the account. It was overly dramatic, probably the most over-the-top competition Mark had ever been involved in. He wouldn't have minded so much, if it didn't put Sophie and himself in such an awful position.

The sister finally looked at him, a curious, measured gaze. Mark wasn't quite sure what to make of it—it wasn't a come-on or anything sexual, more of a sizing up. Then the sister turned to Sophie's mom. "Come on, let's go get some air."

"I don't want any air," the mother snapped.

"We'll make it short," the sister said persuasively, tugging her mom to her feet. "If you stay here and re-view every detail of our offer, you'll drive Sophie nuts. Come on, the walk will do you good. Sophie, you'll be all right, here?"

"Sure," Sophie said, and with that, the two other women walked out the door, leaving Sophie alone with Mark. Mark could've sworn he saw the sister shoot him one more meaningful look, followed by one at Sophie. She did everything but nod her head at Sophie.

Go talk to her, idiot, the expression seemed to say.

"Sophie," Mark said, approaching her cautiously. "I've missed you."

He hadn't meant to open with that, but it was true, so he left it alone. She didn't look at him. "I miss you, too," she replied, staring at her organizer as if it had the secrets of the universe written in it.

"At least it'll all be over today," Mark said. "Then…no matter what happens, it'll be behind us. We can start over."

"I'd like that," Sophie said. "But…Mark, I never did tell you why this is so important to me, did I?"

Mark shrugged, feeling prickles of unease start to creep across his nerve endings. "You're a talented, driven, successful businesswoman," he said. "And I know this is a family business, and a start-up. Of course you'll want to do well."

"My father left my mother a few years before Trimera fired her," Sophie said, and Mark felt ice form in the pit of his stomach. "He'd cleaned out most of her accounts and run up her credit cards. She had to clear out her retirement account to stave off bankruptcy."

"I'm sorry," Mark said inanely, sensing where this was going.

"Then Trimera dumped her before she could even start to build back what she'd lost," Sophie continued.

Mark sighed. "That's terrible," he said. "But…Sophie, layoffs happen. It wasn't personal."

Now Sophie looked at him, her eyes wide and hurt. "It is to the person who gets fired, Mark."

He felt like a worm. "That wasn't what I meant. You know it wasn't."

"That's been our problem," Sophie said, standing and pacing. "I thought that business wasn't personal. I thought we could be one thing in the conference room and another in the bedroom. But it all blends together, Mark." She stood in front of him, crossing her arms. "If we don't get this account, I don't know how we're going to replenish my mom's retirement fund. A lot is riding on the success of this business. And it's not about pride, or being successful. It's more personal than that."

Mark swallowed hard. "I'm not just…" He stopped. "All right. Pride does have a lot to do with why I'm doing this. But damn it, it's also my job, Sophie. I can't ignore doing my job because I feel sorry for your mom."

"I'm not asking you to," Sophie retorted. "But I am trying to tell you that this isn't cut and dried." She took a deep breath. "I want to be with you. You have to know that. But…people are going to get hurt. No matter what the outcome of the business side is, you can't tell me that there won't be consequences."

"We've been over this," Mark said, suddenly not caring that Simone was a few feet outside the door, that Roger was pacing nearby in the hall. "You know what? I hope we don't get the account. I hope that you and your family get exactly what they want. Because I think I'm in love with you, Sophie. And that's worth a hell of a lot more than a stupid promotion."

Sophie's eyes widened and her lip trembled.

Mark couldn't help himself. He leaned down and kissed her sweet, mobile mouth the way he'd been dreaming of since the last time he'd held her in his arms. She kissed him back, softly at first, then with increasingly more abandon. Her hands clutched at his shoulders, and he pulled her to him tightly.

"Mark," she breathed as she pulled away. "I think…"

Before she could finish her sentence, the door opened.

"We're back…" the sister said, before stopping short. Her mouth dropped open in a little *O* of surprise.

"Lydia, don't stop in a doorway like that," her mother

said irritably, stepping around her. She stopped, too, when she took in the sight in front of her: Mark and Sophie, arms around each other, obviously too close to be anything but intimate. "Sophie, what the hell are you doing?"

Sophie took a step away from Mark, her cheeks reddening. "Mom, let me explain…."

"You can't tell me you have an explanation for this!"

"Mrs. Jones, it isn't what you think," Mark interrupted.

The woman turned on him with all the fury of a volcano. She stood in front of him, eyes snapping, so similar to Sophie's, but filled with more anger and bitterness. "I know about you, Mr. McMann," she said. "You make a practice of sleeping with competitors, distributors…anybody you need. And I thought my own daughter was smarter than this, damn it, but I guess with your good looks even she couldn't turn you down." The look of contempt she sent over to Sophie was withering.

"That's not true," Mark said bluntly. Before he could continue, Roger and Simone walked in. "We'll discuss this later."

"There's nothing to discuss." Sophie's mom looked ready to punch someone. "I knew Trimera would stop at nothing to screw me over."

"Now, now, no need to get so personal," Roger said, his tone aghast.

"You don't even know the beginning of the term *personal*," Mrs. Jones answered. "You people would need to be *human* first, to understand how something could be *personal!*"

"Mom," Sophie said, trying to quiet her. Lydia, the sister, looked horrified.

Mrs. Marion and Lily walked into the middle of this circus. Mrs. Marion watched with curiosity, but no alarm. Lily looked a little freaked out by the drama unfolding in front of them.

"If I'm not interrupting," Mrs. Marion said with an edge of sarcasm, causing all the turmoil to disappear momentarily. "I would like to say that, while it's not quite final, we've made a decision."

The room went tomb silent in a nanosecond. Every person listened eagerly. Mark felt his stomach clench.

God as my witness, I have no idea which way I want this to go.

"I have to tell you, it was a very difficult decision," Mrs. Marion said, obviously relishing drawing out the suspense. She was a born showman. Or show-woman. "Diva Nation obviously has the most innovative and creative product, with quality that is second to none. But Trimera…well, the concessions offered were far too sweet to be ignored."

Mark looked over at the Diva Nation team. Sophie didn't look surprised. Her mother looked venomous.

"So, while it's not quite final…we will be drawing up paperwork to start a partnership with Trimera."

Mark shut his eyes, ignoring the clap on his shoulder and Roger's quick word of congratulations, or Simone's gloating little smile. He was about to get everything he'd struggled for years to get. He was finally being taken seriously.

When he opened his eyes, he saw Sophie, looking devastated, next to her mother and her sister.

"I'd like to thank both teams for participating in our challenges…."

Mrs. Marion made her polite speech, but it was obvious that no one was listening. When she drew to a close and walked out, Sophie's mother approached Mark and his team.

"I hope you're happy," she spat out, then turned and stalked out, her daughters following her.

"Jeez," Roger said. "Some people should not be in business. I wonder if we fired her because of her temper?"

"No, we fired her because she was too old," Simone corrected. "At least, we thought she was."

Mark rubbed his hands over his face. "We could be sued for talk like that," he said. "We *should* be sued, if that's what we fired her for."

"Now, now, let's not say the s-word," Roger said, laughing. "Besides, why are you taking that nutcase's side, anyway? We won, they lost, that's life in the big city."

"It was just business," Mark said, his tone slightly mocking.

"Exactly." Roger sounded relieved. "Well, the account's yours, Mark. Keep handling it this well, and in the next year or so, you *will* need to order new business cards!"

Roger laughed as the three of them exited the conference room. Simone tapped Mark on the shoulder. "I told you to cool it with Sophie," she said. "But I guess it all worked out. You landed the account, you'll get the promotion, and it looks like from here on, you've got nothing to worry about."

"What makes you say that?" From what Mark could see, worries were all he had on his horizon.

Simone's laugh was mocking. "Because nobody'll ever find out you were involved with the enemy. I don't think you'll ever hear from Sophie Jones or Diva Nation again if your life depended on it."

SOPHIE FELT DISEMBODIED, as if the whole thing were a dream. The three of them, Lydia, Sophie and their mother, were sitting in the back of a cab, heading at a breakneck pace to their hotel. Lydia sat in between them, trying to act as a buffer. Sophie's mother kept looking down at her purse, as if that accessory somehow held the answers to what had just happened to her. She refused to speak to either of her daughters, despite their best efforts.

"I never told Mark anything about Diva Nation," Sophie said, hoping to pierce through her mother's wall of sadness. "Whatever else happened, we didn't lose because of my…involvement with him."

Her mother looked at her once, a mournful look, but didn't say anything.

Sophie's anger warred with the guilt that was threatening to suffocate her. "Mom, it's not over yet. And we didn't lose the account because I was sleeping with Mark McMann!"

"No, *we* didn't lose the account," her mother finally

said, as the cab stopped in front of their hotel. "*You* lost the account, Sophie."

Sophie felt the rebuke like a slap. Lydia paid the cabbie, and Sophie followed her mother at a run. Her mother pounded the elevator button then crossed her arms.

"It wasn't the greatest idea," Lydia interjected, "but it wasn't her fault, Mom. It was one of those things."

"One of those things?" their mother asked, bewildered. "Just 'one of those things' is a run in your stocking. This was deliberate stupidity."

"Mom," Sophie protested.

"You would take her side, Lydia," her mother continued. "I swear, sometimes I don't know what happened to either of you. I certainly didn't raise you this way." She glowered. "It must be your father. He was selfish, too."

"Hey, whoa, wait a minute," Lydia said, putting her hands up. "I wasn't screwing the competition, here."

"Lydia!"

"Sorry, Sophie," Lydia added. "You know what I meant."

Sophie felt like tearing out her hair in frustration. When the three of them were in the elevator, she repeated, in a soft voice, "Mom, what happened with Mark really didn't have anything to do with it."

"You honestly believe that, don't you?" Her mother shook her head. "You think that being infatuated with the man you're competing against didn't make you lose your edge? They play dirty over there, and I needed you to be just as tough as they were." She paused, looking at Sophie with derision. "They must have seen you coming a mile away."

"I'm not stupid." Sophie felt tears edging out of her eyes, and she wiped them carefully with her fingertips.

"You slept with a man who was directly competing with you," her mother countered quietly. "You chose to let your focus go. You weren't even discreet about it." The elevator doors opened, and her mother stepped out. "If that wasn't stupid, Sophie, I don't know what is."

"That's not fair." Sophie crossed her arms. "I worked my hardest on this. I put in long hours, I did the research, I did everything I possibly could. And maybe we lost, but I tried."

"Yeah. You tried." Her mother threw her purse down on the hotel-room bed. "And yet your lover will get the account. Tell me, do you really think he's going to see you again after he wins it?"

Sophie felt a pang. The question had crossed her own mind.

He said he was falling in love with me. But did he mean it?

Her mother rubbed at her temples. "Sophie, talking about this won't help any. I am too angry with you to speak to you, and it's not going to be better. So be silent, or get out of here."

Sophie felt something inside of her snap. "Mom, all my life, you've been the logical one. The disciplinarian. The one who always told us what to do and when we weren't good enough…"

Her mother sat down on the bed, next to her purse. "I am too tired for this, Sophie. I do not want to have to go into a 'why Sophie's life is terrible' conversation. This wasn't about *you*. This was about me!"

"It's still about you!" Sophie stood in front of her mother, her heart racing in her chest. "You saw how many hours I put into this. You saw what I sacrificed to make this happen!"

"Obviously not enough!"

"Even if I hadn't slept with Mark, we wouldn't have won the account!"

Her mother stared at her as if she'd been slapped. "That's a lie," her mother said, her voice shaking. "The products were impeccable. The only way Trimera could win was by playing dirty…."

"Which they *would have done anyway*," Sophie pointed out. "Whether I was with Mark or not. We don't have the money to fight them, Mom. It was a long shot, and I'm proud we made it as far as we did!"

"You're merely trying to justify what you did," her mother railed. "You're making excuses for your behavior…."

"You know what? It was a bad choice to sleep with Mark. But I will say this—I didn't do a single thing that I'm not proud of."

Her mother's eyes widened. "You're proud of sabotaging our chances?"

"I'm proud of the work I did, and I'm proud of loving Mark."

There. She'd said it. She couldn't believe she'd admitted it out loud, but it was too late to take it back, and she was filled with enough righteous anger that she wouldn't have taken it back given the opportunity.

"Love?" Her mother's scorn was evident. She got to her feet. "You *are* stupid, if you believe that!"

Sophie stood her ground.

"So that's it, then." Her mother's eyes filled with tears. "You've chosen an outsider, some *man,* over your own family. Well, that's fine."

"It doesn't have to be an exclusive choice, Mom," Sophie said, the tears she was seeing bothering her more than any of her mother's hurtful words. "I didn't choose him over you guys."

"Get out."

"Mom?"

"Get out!" Her mother opened the door. "You think that your choices don't have consequences? Well, if you're so proud of what you did, and you love this man so much, then go stay with *him!*"

"Mom," Lydia interrupted. "Come on. You don't mean that. You're upset…."

"You're damned right I'm upset, Lydia, and you stay out of this! This is between your sister and me!"

Sophie grabbed her roller bag from its place in the corner of the room. "Fine. I'll leave."

"Mom, Sophie, this is crazy," Lydia said. "It's just business, after all!"

Her mother did not budge from her place at the open

door, continuing to hold it open. Sophie rolled past her. "I am sorry," she said.

Her mother didn't respond, so Sophie kept on walking.

Lydia followed after her. "Mom doesn't mean it," Lydia tried. "She's angry, you know how much this meant to her…."

"I screwed up," Sophie replied. "But I didn't deserve that."

"I know."

They walked in silence for a second, until they got to the elevator. "So what are you going to do?" Lydia asked.

Sophie was wondering that, herself. "I'll think of something."

"Mom will probably try to change flights, get out of here tonight instead of tomorrow, cancel the hotel room." Lydia sounded concerned.

"I'll stay on tomorrow's flight." No sense in continuing the family dramatics while trapped on a cross-country flight, after all. "And I'll stay somewhere else tonight."

"With Mark?"

Sophie closed her eyes. She didn't know if it was making things worse, but she needed to find out if he still meant what he'd said: that he was falling in love with her.

I'm not choosing him over my family, she told herself doggedly. *I'm choosing my own life. I did my best—now, I need to see if this has a chance.*

MARK WAITED IMPATIENTLY. After Simone's snide remark, he was debating with himself how he could convince Sophie to forgive him and to continue their relationship. Then, out of nowhere, she'd called him, asking if she could stay at his apartment. He'd agreed willingly, thinking it was the perfect opportunity for them to get some things hashed out.

If everything works out, he thought, *I could have it all. The account...the girl. Everything.* It was almost too much to hope for.

Mark opened his door to find Sophie there, looking wrecked. Her makeup was mostly rubbed away, presumably from crying. She looked young, tired and vulnerable.

"Oh, God, Sophie. What happened?"

"Can I come in?" she asked instead, in a small voice.

"Of course." He took her roller bag and ushered her inside, putting an arm around her shoulders and giving her a comforting squeeze. "Can I get you anything? Something to drink, maybe?"

"I don't drink much ordinarily," she said, then barked out a short, bitter laugh. "But today's far from ordinary. Sure, I'll have a shot of whatever you've got."

He guided her to his sofa, then quickly fetched her a short glass of scotch. "It's all I've got in the house," he offered.

He expected her to sip it. Instead, she took a manful slug of it, coughing explosively afterward. "Thanks," she said when she regained her breath.

"Okay, talk to me." He sat next to her, taking the glass from her hands and putting it on the coffee table, out of her reach. "This isn't because of the damned Marion & Co. account, is it?"

"Yes, and no." She took a deep, unsteady breath. "This is because of the account, but it's more about you and me."

He was afraid of that. "We didn't…"

"I know, I know," she interrupted. "I used the same arguments. But my mother was upset, and to be honest, she was right. Deep down, I knew how important this was to my family. I knew that on some level, getting involved with you would jeopardize our chances. I knew all of that, and I chose you anyway."

He swallowed hard against the knot in his throat. "But you didn't lose the account because of me," he said staunchly, desperate to convince her. To convince them both, really.

She leaned over, putting her hand against the side of his face. "The point is, even knowing that…I'm still choosing you. I wouldn't be here right now if I didn't."

He was humbled by the admission. Turning his face, he pressed a heated kiss into her palm. "I love you, Sophie," he breathed. "And I hate to see you hurting like this. Especially because of me."

"Then help me forget."

She reached for him, her eyes full of need and sadness. He stood, tugging her to her feet. Then with great tenderness he swept her up, lifting her as though she weighed nothing, and carried her to his bedroom. He placed her on the bed gently. "Sophie," he murmured, kissing her before releasing her. Slowly, he took off his shirt. She simply watched him, so he reached for her, helping her out of her clothing. He removed her jacket and unbuttoned her silk blouse with fingers that trembled. He'd had sex plenty of times in his past—and he'd had incredible, scorching-hot sex with Sophie, for that matter. But somehow, this time, it all seemed different and new. It meant more. This time wasn't clandestine—they weren't sneaking around, and the specter of business no longer loomed over them. They weren't pretending this was "just one night" that didn't mean anything, that didn't affect them. She'd chosen him, she'd said. As far as he was concerned, this was the beginning of forever.

He kissed her neck as he stripped the blouse away, and she threaded her fingers into the hair at the nape of his neck, holding him tightly against her. He bit her skin delicately, then sucked, hard enough to leave a mark. She gasped but didn't release her hold on him. If anything, she clung tighter.

It had been two weeks since he'd had a chance to talk to her, much less touch her. He wanted to drink her in. In the heated frenzy that was overtaking him, he felt as if he never wanted to be apart from her again. His mind reeled from the impact of that thought.

To get his bearings, he focused on the moment: the feel of her, the scent of her, the taste. He seemed hyper-aware of her. "You're so amazing," he whispered, tugging off her skirt. "So beautiful."

"You make me feel beautiful," she replied. "When you make love to me…I can't explain it. It's magic."

She was now in just her matching black underwear and stockings, complete with garter. He groaned as his body tightened in response to the inviting picture of her, lying on his bed in that state. He broke away from her long enough to strip off the rest of his clothes and roll on a condom. Her gaze devoured his body every second he was away. He dove for her, tenderness starting to slip in the face of an overwhelming hunger.

She obviously felt the same way because the moment he hit the bed she was touching him, her fingers gliding over the planes of his stomach, circling his shaft and stroking it until he groaned and involuntarily pressed forward. She kissed his chest, licking his clavicle lightly before nibbling at his shoulder. The counterpoint of butterfly-light caresses versus the insistent hand closed over his cock was enough to drive him wild. To his surprise, she nudged him onto his back with force.

"I want you," she said, her eyes ablaze with it. "Right now. I want to take you."

"Have I ever said no?" he answered with a rasping laugh.

"It wasn't a question," she said, and he was relieved when she laughed as well. It was a small step, but the grief in her eyes was receding. It was replaced with desire, yes, but something else…something he'd dwell on later, since now she was positioning herself over his taut body, taunting him by slowly edging herself onto him, teasing the tip of his cock with her entrance. Her breathing had gone shallow, and her eyes went half-lidded, her smile slow and bemused.

"You're going to kill me," he said through gritted teeth, after the torture had continued for several minutes.

"You're a big guy. You'll survive," she said, but obligingly she lowered herself more, finally taking in all of him. Feeling the tight clutch of her body circling him forced him to concentrate everything he could on taking his time, not simply gripping her and driving his way toward completion. The feel of her was enough to make him lose his mind if he let her. He struggled, feeling every muscle in his body tense in the battle of willpower versus pleasure.

"Oh, Mark," she said in a low voice as her body moved sinuously over his. His fingers dug into her hips, trying to somehow control her pace and hold her to him. She laughed, her hips moving in with a slight twist that made his eyes cross from sheer sensual overload. "This feels so *good...*"

His breathing was ragged. "Now I know you're going to kill me," he gasped.

"You'll thank me later."

Despite the joking quality in her statement, her face grew serious, her eyes closing as she focused intently on the task at hand. Her breasts jutted out proudly and he shifted his hands to cup them, eliciting a moan of pleasure from her. She pressed forward and he circled her nipples with his thumbs, gratified by her panting gasps of surprised desire. The action made her circle her hips yet again, and he almost lost it. His hips rose to meet the juncture of her thighs.

She leaned down, pressing the full length of her body against his, her hands gripping his shoulders, her legs twining with his and drawing him deeper into her welcoming warmth. Her breathing was now rhythmic and quick, her face drawn in sexual concentration. She was close, he knew it. "Come on, baby," he whispered near her ear, biting her shoulder as he slammed upward, groaning when she moaned and ground her body against his.

"Ah...*ah*..." She threw her head back, her hips moving spasmodically against his. *"Mark!"*

She shuddered over him, and he drove himself into her, relishing in the sensation of her release closing around him. He waited for a full minute as she collapsed against him. It took everything he had not to give in and surrender himself with her. But he wanted this sensation to last.

"That was amazing," she said finally, lifting her head. Then she looked at him, puzzled. "You didn't, though, did you?"

"That one was for you," he said. Then, with one deft motion, he flipped her onto her back, never exiting her body. "We've got all night, Sophie."

All night, and the rest of our lives...

She laughed, and he delighted in the sound. The laugh turned husky as he moved inside her, the slickness of her orgasm making the motion fluid and easy. "I've never wanted anyone the way I want you," he said as he began to move in and out in a simple, continuous motion. The tight feel of her, clenching around him, was like coming home. He had always enjoyed sex, but it had never felt this perfect before. He kissed her shoulders, her neck, the sliding caress of her body beneath his feeling both passionate and yet somehow comforting.

"I've never felt this way," she responded, her legs anchoring themselves over his hips as she rose to meet his every thrust. She arched her back, exposing her neck to his heated kisses. The low, throaty moans that she whispered only seemed to heighten the sensations he was feeling.

She's the most amazing woman, he marveled. *How did I get so lucky?*

They moved as one, rhythmically, as perfectly as a symphony, their bodies in a harmony of heat and beauty. She clutched at his shoulders, and he leaned down, his tongue twining with hers as they kissed deeply, their bodies connected in every way possible.

He gave himself over to her, the snug closeness, the way her every noise and movement seemed to turn him on even more. After a few moments, she was breathing hard again, and he could sense his own climax building.

"Sophie…baby, I'm…"

"Yes," she said, her fingernails raking down his back and causing his pleasure to redouble. "I'm there, I'm going to…"

She cried out, and the sound and the sensation of her body closing around him yet again finally pushed him over the edge. His orgasm ripped through him like a cannonball, and he slammed himself against her willing body with a muted shout of release. For a second, there was absolutely nothing else in the world but her and the sensation exploding through him. He collapsed against her, his heart pounding, the blood rushing in his ears as he struggled for breath.

After long moments, he rolled to his side, still holding her. "That was amazing," he said.

"That is an understatement," she said, laughing. Then she smoothed the hair off his forehead, away from his eyes. "It's always been this way. Indescribable." She shrugged. "I never thought I'd be this insane for great sex."

He knew immediately that, despite his efforts, she'd shifted back to her pain. "You weren't just going crazy for great sex," he reminded her. "Neither was I."

"That's how it started," she reminded him.

He stroked her shoulder. "But that's not how it's ended up."

She still looked worried, he noticed. And the fact that she was forcing herself to smile brightly only made him feel worse.

He traced her cheek with one fingertip, marveling at the softness of her skin. "We won't come up with all the solutions tonight," he said. "But we will come up with something, I promise you."

She nodded, but he could see in her eyes that she didn't quite believe him. After the way the Marion & Co. fiasco had panned out, things hadn't worked out for everyone. They'd worked out for him. They'd simply turned out to be a disaster for her.

"I won't leave you hanging," he continued. "Got that?"

She smiled, but the smile didn't reach her eyes. "Let's just enjoy this weekend," she said. "Then…we'll see what happens."

The guilt he'd felt increased, almost drowning him. He set his jaw. It had just been business, and he hadn't meant to hurt her—but she was hurting. He thought he could chalk it up to bad luck, and continue a relationship with her. But could he do that, knowing he'd damaged her relationships with her family, and cost her her job? Would he ask her to leave everything and move in with him in New York? And, after all that…would she always hold those things against him, even though she claimed not to?

He closed his eyes, holding her to him tightly. He was a problem solver, damn it.

There had to be something else, some better way to do this. He loved her enough—he owed her enough—to find it.

9

SOPHIE SAT IN MARK'S BEDROOM, the dim light pouring in through the half-closed blinds.

So this is what it feels like to be unemployed, she mused, leaning back and stretching. Other than the nagging guilt, it didn't feel that bad. In fact, there was a certain relief to know that in some ways her fate was decided and it was out of her hands.

"How are you feeling?"

She looked up to see Mark, wearing only a robe, carrying a breakfast tray. His hair was mussed, and he looked outrageously sexy.

"I'm famished," she said as he put the tray in front of her.

"It's nothing fancy," he said modestly. "I hope you like cheese omelets, since that's my specialty."

It looked like something a restaurant might serve. He'd even included a small vase with a rose. The omelet looked fluffy, and there was salsa as a garnish. He'd also included buttered toast, a cup of coffee and a glass of orange juice.

"You're spoiling me," she said, smiling at him.

"You deserve to be spoiled," he said, and she wondered offhand if he was still feeling guilty.

"You don't have to do anything for me," she said softly, hoping that he understood she meant more than serving her breakfast.

He sat down next to her. "Maybe I want to," he said, brushing her hair away from her face. "Eat your eggs, before they get cold."

She did, enjoying the savory meal even as she had difficulty swallowing due to the lump in her throat. He was being so kind, so tender. He was in love with her.

How are we going to make this work?

She pushed the thought out of her mind. She wasn't going to think about the competition, or business, or anything but each moment she was living. There was only the present, and she wasn't going to ruin it with stress.

Time enough to worry, she counseled herself, sipping the fresh-squeezed orange juice. *I may not have a chance like this again.*

She shut her eyes. She didn't want to think about her relationship with Mark ending, but there it was…creeping into her consciousness, hovering at the edge of all of her thoughts.

She opened her eyes to find Mark staring at her. "You're doing it again," he said.

"Doing what?" she said as he took the breakfast tray away and put it on a nearby desk.

"You're thinking about what happened."

She tried for a smile, but it came out halfhearted. "It just happened, Mark," she said. "I've got to fly back today, and I'll be dealing with the fallout then." She raised her chin resolutely. "But we've still got a few hours, right?"

Now he looked somber. She leaned forward, reaching for the belt of his robe. "Mark," she said, tugging the knot loose. "I'll be honest with you. I don't know how much time we have together."

Before he could protest her statement, his robe fell open, revealing his glorious nakedness. *I can't get enough of this man,* she thought with a smile, pushing aside the covers to reveal her own naked body. She was gratified when he studied her, his frown turning into a smile.

"We've got plenty of time, Sophie," he said in a thick voice as she helped him shrug out of his robe.

"I know," she reassured him. "So let's enjoy it."

She kissed the rough stubble starting to grow on his chiseled chin, moving down to the hard column of his neck. Her fingers twined in his hair, delighting in the messy waves. He growled and buried his face against her shoulder, nuzzling her. She laughed, feeling some of the stress bunching up her muscles start to ease.

His hands smoothed down the planes of her sides, resting on her hips as he kissed first one nipple, then the other, before slowly drawing it into his mouth. She gasped as he suckled, slowly, causing waves of sensation to radiate through her in growing circles. She arched up to meet him, her fingers clutching at the yoke of his shoulders. "Mark," she breathed, the single syllable infused with happiness and longing.

He smiled, that devilish, mischievous smile that was undoubtedly her favorite. "Hold on a sec," he said, then his mouth moved lower, pressing heated kisses against her stomach as his hands moved lower....

She jolted in surprise when he parted her legs with his long, agile fingers, pressing into her warm heat slowly. He kissed down to her curls, his breath heating her most sensitive junction. She felt her heartbeat beginning to pound in an increasing rhythm. She gasped as she felt his tongue dip inside her, tracing her folds with gentle insistence.

She leaned back, all rational thought fleeing in the face of his sensuous onslaught. Her fingers dug into the sheets, her hands bunching into fists as he slowly worked his magic, his tongue and mouth swirling against her. She felt the beginnings of her climax start to build, and her breathing turned to gasps, as she tossed her head back and forth, desperate to hold on to some semblance of control.

He moved his mouth, and she almost whimpered against the loss of his hot breath when she felt his fingers penetrate her, even as his tongue manipulated her clit. The orgasm hit her like a lightning bolt, sudden and unexpected, and she cried out, slamming her head against the thick pillow reflexively.

When the last rippling aftershocks of the climax dissipated, she looked up to find him grinning at her smugly.

"That was incredible," she said, blinking slowly, slightly out of breath.

"I'm glad," he said, and she giggled at his look of almost arrogant satisfaction.

"Pretty pleased with yourself, aren't you?"

He leaned down, kissing her shoulders, her collarbone, the hollow between her breasts. "Pretty pleased with *us*," he corrected.

"Us," she echoed. "Has a nice ring to it."

His eyes were glowing with warmth. "Ready to talk about it?"

Just like that, the stress that had been effectively banished from her now desire-sated body crept back like a thief, infiltrating every muscle. Before she could answer, he sighed.

"Sophie, we can't ignore the situation."

She bit her lip. "Have you come up with an answer that will help my family and my company, and give you the promotion you deserve?"

He started to say something, then shut his mouth with a click. He shook his head. "Not yet, anyway," he conceded. "But not talking about it won't get us any closer to an answer."

She set her chin mutinously. "I don't need you to solve my problems, Mark. I got myself into this mess."

He rolled her onto him, the feel of his heated skin beneath hers seeping into her like the warmth of a hot-rock massage. She melted onto him, her legs splaying out. She felt the tip of his cock tickle at her still-damp entrance, and her heart skipped a beat.

"This isn't a mess," he said, his eyes solemn. "It's not a great situation, but I can't be sorry I met you."

He pushed into her, parting her…filling her. She moaned softly as he withdrew, sliding against her, causing the already sensitive skin to tremble with pleasure.

"I can't be sorry we have this," he said, his voice thick. He pressed into her again, his hips slowly arching up to meet hers. She gyrated slowly, swiveling her hips to feel him more deeply inside her, and he groaned.

"I'm not sorry we have this, either," she said as he covered her breasts with his hands, stroking her nipples. She raised her hips up and then lowered them again, savoring the feeling of his long, hard cock inside her.

He groaned, and she could feel the tension in his muscles, corded beneath her palms. She started to increase her tempo, surprised to feel another orgasm starting its incremental build inside her.

I want this forever, she thought as he smoothed his hands to her hips, pulling her to him, burying himself in her. She leaned down, her breasts dragging across his chest as their bodies slid against each other. He bit her shoulder gently, and she twined her legs with his, molding herself to him…keeping him deeply inside her as they rocked against each other.

His breathing went harsh and ragged, and he rolled her onto her back, his thrusts becoming powerful, insistent. She clenched her thighs, eager to hold him, almost desperate in her need. She felt the climax shimmer through her, and she cried out just as he groaned, his hips bucking against hers as her body clenched him.

After long moments, he collapsed against her, the thin sheen of sweat from their bodies making them slick. She could feel his hot breath against her neck, smell his woodsy, purely masculine scent surrounding her.

I want this forever, she thought again. Not only the passion, but the aftermath. The feeling of comfort. The feeling of hope, and security. Something beyond work.

She wanted love.

He kissed her throat. "We have to make this happen," he rasped. "I'll think of something."

She tried hard to focus on her thoughts. She was too used to taking care of herself to simply wait while someone else handled the problem.

"We'll think of something," she corrected, and ignored the tension that invariably crept back into her body. "Don't worry. We'll think of something."

SOPHIE STEELED HERSELF TO GO back to her mother's house. Sophie had spent the time before at Mark's place, trying futilely to come up with some kind of solution. She'd tried calling her mother, but there had been no answer, and Sophie really hadn't expected one. If she was going to patch this up, it would have to be on her mother's home turf, at her home. She just hoped that her mother wasn't in full-entrenchment mode. She'd gotten that way after Sophie's father had left, and when Trimera had fired her. Sophie certainly didn't want to be lumped in that category.

"She's not taking it well," Lydia had said, when Sophie had called. "She's not talking to me, either. And she's in a real depression. I haven't seen her this bad, even when Trimera canned her."

That made Sophie feel even worse. Even though she hadn't done anything wrong, technically, she still felt responsible. Sophie didn't know where her future was heading, but she had to fix this. Her family meant too much to her to simply walk away, claiming innocence.

She opened her mom's door. "Mom?"

She found her in the kitchen, still in her bathrobe despite the fact it was one o'clock in the afternoon. She was sipping a cup of coffee. There were papers strewn around, obviously notes about the Marion & Co. product line. Sophie felt her stomach sink to the floor. Her mom looked up. "What are you doing here?" she asked, her voice flat.

"Mom," Sophie said, sitting at the kitchen table next to her. "I came here to see if I could put things right between us."

Her mother frowned. "There's nothing to fix, Sophie. It's all over."

"You can't mean that," Sophie said, feeling bereft. "I made a mistake, yes, but I'm sorry and I don't want you to…to cut me out of your life for it!"

Her mother seemed to finally focus in on Sophie

after that statement. "No, no, Sophie," she corrected. "I didn't mean…the Marion & Co. issue is all over. It's impossible to put right. That's what I meant."

"So…we're all right?"

"I'm not thrilled with you now, no," her mother answered. "But you're my daughter, and I love you. And I can't blame you. As tough and street smart as you like to think you are—baby, you're still naive when it comes to business."

Sophie bit her lip. Things were on the road to recovery—she wasn't about to ruin that, simply because she felt insulted by her mother's patronizing air.

"You got snowed," her mother continued, pausing to sip her coffee. "I should've expected it. I'm surprised it wasn't worse, actually." Her eyes narrowed. "Did you see him again?"

"Yes." Sophie's gaze didn't waver. She didn't want to ruin things, true, but she also wasn't going to lie about Mark.

"Do you expect to continue in a relationship with this guy?"

"Yes."

"I'll bet he's as surprised about it as you are," her mother said.

Sophie gritted her teeth. "Mom, he never set out to use me."

"I won't argue with you about it. It's too late now anyway," her mother said with a shrug. "I suppose you're moving to New York to be closer to him, then?"

Sophie glanced down at the tabletop. "We're still discussing what we're going to do," she said. Then, because she couldn't help herself, she asked, "What makes you think he wouldn't move out here?"

"He's already made it clear that his career comes before you, and his job's in New York," her mother pointed out. "And you don't have anything holding you here, so it seemed logical."

Sophie swallowed hard. "So…you're firing me, then? Just…cutting me off?"

Her mother's eyes were sad. "Sophie, honey, I know I was mad at you. And I'm still disappointed. But I love you. I'm not cutting you off. I'm simply trying to be reasonable."

Sophie had steeled herself for her mother's anger. Her understanding and the compassion in her voice were unexpected. Sophie felt tears start to well up in her eyes, and she cleared her throat. "If you're not mad at me, why can't I still work with you?" She wiped at the corner of her eyes with her fingertips. "I know this was a big deal. But we can get other deals. We were starting to really get some traction at the sales conferences. If we work even harder—especially if we use some of the new stuff you developed—then I'm sure we can somehow turn it around…."

"Sophie, it's over," her mother said. "This was it. If we didn't get the Marion account, then we were going to go under."

"Things are tight, granted…"

"I took out a second mortgage on the house."

Sophie goggled. "Why didn't you tell me?"

"You may be my business whiz kid, but there were some things I didn't think you needed to know," her mother said with a tone of injured dignity. "I didn't want you to have the pressure of that, on top of everything else you were doing. Besides, you probably would've tried to stop me."

"You're damned right I would have!" Sophie said, aghast. "How are you going to carry those payments?"

Her mother made a small sweeping gesture with her hand. "I've been meaning to downsize anyway."

"You mean…you're losing your *house?*"

"I knew what I was getting into," her mother replied. "Sophie, you have your own life and you made your own choices. I'm not putting the blame for this on you. I counted on this too much, I guess."

It was impossible for Sophie to feel lower. She wanted to weep. "I didn't know," she said, seeing how her mother must have felt betrayed. The Marion account meant far more than Sophie had realized, and it had already meant a lot. Now, with the closing of Diva Nation, her mother's retirement and now her home were disappearing. "This… Oh, God, Mom, this can't happen."

"What are you going to do?" her mother asked. "Sophie, it's a lost cause."

"You must hate me," Sophie said.

"Let's not get melodramatic. I've already told you how I feel," her mother said briskly. "Now, I'm working on putting it behind me. I never should've put myself in the position where I could be screwed by Trimera again. I need to pick up the pieces and move on."

"There's got to be a way to undo this," Sophie said, racking her brain.

"Sophie, knock it off." Her mother stood up, shuffling in her slippers and pouring herself another cup of coffee. "I leaned too hard on my girls, that's all."

"I wanted to help you!" Sophie protested. "I wouldn't have done all this if I didn't!"

"You were in over your head," her mother said. "Admit it, Sophie. You love me, but you didn't fathom just how bad this would be. And as you said, you made your choices. I'm not saying that this guy is the devil. I'm saying—in the clutch, you chose him. Live with that."

Sophie nodded, but her chest ached. She'd said as much to Mark—that she'd chosen him. She loved him; she craved him. But here, in the light of her mother's kitchen, hearing about the consequences, she felt petty and selfish and wrong.

"I wish I could make this up to you," Sophie said.

"Yeah, well, if you come up with anything, let me know," her mother said, and the knife twisted deeper into Sophie's heart. "In the meantime…I need to call a real estate agent this afternoon."

Sophie watched as her mother went down the hallway, coffee cup in hand. Sophie looked around at all the product notes and samples that littered every horizontal surface.

She grabbed up her cell phone and dialed Mark. "Hey you," he answered immediately. "How's it going? How are you holding up?"

Sophie quickly outlined the problem. "She's losing her house, Mark. I have to do something."

Mark sighed over the crackle of cell reception. "I don't know what I can do, Sophie," he said, his voice rich with regret.

"Isn't there some other account that we could land?" Sophie pleaded. "You know the industry, all the ins and outs. You know who's buying!"

"I can give you the names of a few distributors," Mark said. "But…it's not going to be easy, and it'll take time. You guys are aiming too high. If you had a few years…"

"But she doesn't. I need to make a mint in a hurry," Sophie said quickly.

"I'm so sorry," Mark said.

Sophie closed her eyes. "It's all right," she said. "It's not your problem."

"Sophie, don't…"

"I didn't mean it like that," she said. "But it is our company. And one way or another, we'll figure out a way around it."

He sighed heavily. "I really am sorry."

"I know." She glanced at her watch. "I have to go."

"When can I see you again?"

"I'll be in New York to sort out some final things for Diva Nation," she said. "We'll be together then."

"I miss you," he said.

"Miss you, too," she replied. "I really have to go."

He paused, then hung up.

She sat there for a second, feeling numb. Her mother would lose her house. Her company would go under. And as much as he loved her, Mark could not help her.

She had to help herself.

She picked up her cell phone, dialing carefully. "Marion & Co.," the voice said cheerfully on the other line.

"I need to talk to Mrs. Abigail Marion," Sophie said.

"May I ask who is calling?"

"Tell her that Sophie Jones from Diva Nation is calling," Sophie said slowly. "Tell her I have a deal for her."

10

"So WHAT DID YOU WANT to set up this meeting for, Mark?" Roger said, sitting in his office. "I've only got about twenty minutes, by the way. I'm meeting with the CEO on the links at eleven."

"I appreciate the time," Mark said. Simone was sitting next to him, opposite Roger's broad glass desk. She looked puzzled, too. "This is about the Marion & Co. account."

"You did a great job," Roger said. "Surprised the hell out of me. Not just me, either." He smiled, a broad, used-car salesman type smile. "If you're worried about getting the job, don't be. You earned it. I'll be sure you get that promotion."

"That's good to know," Mark said, savoring the satisfaction of the words for a second before plowing forward. "What I wanted to say was…Diva Nation did a great job, though. They came damned close."

Roger shrugged. "I don't follow."

Mark swallowed, surprised to find himself nervous. He hadn't felt this way since his first runway show, back when he was seventeen years old. But this was a big risk for him.

She's worth it.

"I was thinking," Mark said cautiously. "It'd be a terrible waste for Diva Nation to fall off the map completely."

Roger frowned, puzzled. Simone's eyes widened, Mark noticed.

"I would like the ability to hire Sophie," he said.

Simone shook her head almost imperceptibly. Mark kept going.

"And I think it's a damned shame we fired Mrs. Jones, the chemist," Mark said. "After all, she's the one who came up with those products. We really could use someone that innovative. I think she's adequately proven that her age isn't a factor."

Roger was now bewildered. "You're saying…you want to *hire* the competition? Is that it?"

Mark nodded, trying hard to look casual. "I think it'd be a smart business move."

Roger, to Mark's surprise, burst out laughing. "Christ, kid," he muttered. "You know, maybe I was too hasty in telling you the promotion was in the bag."

Mark blanched. "I won that account," he protested.

"Yeah, and now you're trying to snatch defeat from the jaws of victory. They're bush league," Roger said dismissively. "We can't save all the orphans and lost puppies in the world, Mark. Life's hard. If they want to play against the big boys, they're just going to have to get hurt." Roger crossed his arms, studying Mark curiously. "I would've thought you knew that by now."

"What I'm saying isn't personal," Mark said, glad that his voice was cold and dispassionate. "It's that…Sophie Jones is a good exec, and her Mom is a good chemist. There should be a place for them at Trimera. We hire people all the time."

"Yeah, but not people we've slept with."

Mark winced at Simone's words, feeling the blood chill in his veins. He glanced at her; she was glaring at him. "This isn't—"

"Listen, I already told you I have a tee time set up," Roger said, "so I'll make this brief. No, we cannot save your girlfriend. No, we cannot save her mom. We won, they lost. You all need to deal with it." Roger stood up, gesturing to the door. "You know, Mark, talks like this really don't encourage me. I thought that you had gained more business sense than that. But this only convinces me that you're still using your body more than your head."

Mark grimaced, feeling rage bubble through him. He nodded curtly and left, Simone following him all the way to his office. She shut the door behind them, then lashed out at him. *"Are you crazy?"*

"I guess I am," he spat back, feeling humiliated.

"You stuck your neck out for some rinky-dink competitor that you've been sleeping with," Simone growled. "I thought I taught you better than this. People have been telling me you're some pretty-boy model, that you've been coasting along on my coattails. But I stood up for you because I thought you had the killer instinct, and that you had a brain in that gorgeous head of yours. And now, this is the thanks I get?"

"So sorry, Simone," he said sharply. "I didn't realize how much I was going to injure *you* in this whole deal."

She let out a long exhalation. "You fell in love with her, didn't you?"

He clenched his jaw, refusing to answer.

"Well, that's just peachy," she said sarcastically. "Good luck getting taken seriously now, sport. And I wouldn't bank on that promotion, either."

Mark felt his gut knot into a cold ball of stress. "Why not?"

"Because you blew it," Simone said. "Frankly, you were always a dark horse for it, but we all thought that maybe you were finally showing some progress. Now, I think you're right back to square one."

"I showed that I knew my stuff," Mark said. "We wouldn't even have the account if you'd left Carol on it all by herself."

"That might be the case," Simone said, returning to her usual icy-calm demeanor. "But that was then. Carol could easily run the new account, now that you've landed it for us."

Mark gaped. After everything he'd done…all that work…all the problems with Sophie, they were going to simply hang him out to dry?

"It doesn't have to happen this way," Simone said. "But seriously, given the same opportunity, do you truly think your girlfriend over at Diva Nation would turn her back on landing the account? It's huge. It would make or break them." Simone shook her head. "It's not personal. It's just business, Mark."

"I don't believe that," he said staunchly. Sophie had already given up too much, made too many sacrifices because of how she felt about him. And he knew how she felt about big corporations.

"You don't have to," Simone said. "But mark my words, when it comes down to it, you'd be surprised what people will do when it comes to business."

He watched, depressed, as she walked out. He picked up his phone to call Sophie—needing to hear her voice, and feel a bit better about the situation. He stopped himself before he could hit Send, though. He hadn't told her about what he'd been planning to do. Unfortunately, it had been the only solution to their problem that he could think of. Their business would still fail. Her mother's retirement would still be in jeopardy. They'd still be living on opposite coasts. And if it became widely known that they were involved, he got the feeling that Roger would probably make him pay for it, one way or another.

Somehow, he'd managed to make the situation even worse for himself.

He dialed her anyway. "Mark," she said, and he felt a little of the tension ebb away.

"I wanted to hear your voice," he replied.

"You sound sad," she said. "Not going well, huh?"

"You could say that." *You could also say that things are a flaming, complete and utter disaster.*

"Don't worry," Sophie said, obviously trying to reassure him.

"Well, keep your chin up," he told her, more to buck himself up than her. "No matter what happens on the business side, we'll still have each other, right?"

There was a long pause on the other end of the line. "I love you," she murmured.

He felt warmth blossom in his chest. "I love you, too," he said. "I'll call you tonight."

He hung up, then stared at the phone for a long minute. She wouldn't screw him over, he thought.

But his own company, he realized…now, that was a different story. They didn't think he could make it. They didn't believe in him.

Maybe, he mused, *I need to think outside the box on this one.*

He mulled it over, then picked up the phone. "I'd like to speak to Mrs. Abigail Marion, please. Tell her it's Mark McMann from Trimera."

There was a click as he was transferred. Then he heard Mrs. Marion's smooth voice.

"Mark," she said, almost gleeful. "I've been expecting to hear from you."

"IT'S GOOD TO SEE YOU, MARK," Mrs. Marion said warmly, gesturing him into her office. "It was a very difficult decision, I don't mind telling you. Still, I'm sure that with the package Trimera is offering, I wouldn't find better anywhere in the marketplace."

Mark sat across from Mrs. Marion's broad teak desk, frowning slightly. He'd been racking his brain for the past twenty-four hours, getting almost no sleep in the process.

This is all because you got involved with Sophie Jones. Ever since he'd decided to give Sophie a ride, his life had changed irrevocably. Now, he was on the brink of the biggest coup of his career…and he was about to jeopardize all of it, for her.

You can do this.

He cleared his throat. "Trimera did offer amazing terms," he said. "You know, we never would have been able to offer you that many perks and benefits if it weren't for such a large account. And of course, Trimera's a multimillion-dollar company."

Her smile was puzzled. "Mark, I already said yes to Trimera. You can stop selling."

"The thing is…the products won't be as good as Diva Nation's."

Her eyes widened at his admission. "Yes. That was a consideration," she said carefully. "But you assured me you could make similar products."

"Knock-offs are always inferior to the original," he said, even as a part of him wondered just what Simone and Roger would say if they knew what he was up to. "And Diva Nation is definitely onto something, with their palette, their cosmetic ingredients…"

He let the sentence peter off as Mrs. Marion held a hand up, halting him.

"Mark, what exactly are you trying to do here?" Her

voice was calm, but her eyes were shrewd. "Because if I didn't know better, I'd swear you're trying to get rid of our business."

"No, not at all," Mark said hastily. This was where it got tricky. "Trimera definitely wants your business, and you won't be able to get a better deal anywhere, as you said."

"So why do you keep bringing up Diva Nation?"

"Because it's not their fault that they couldn't compete," he said candidly. His business-school teachers would be wincing over his negotiation style. Hell, part of him felt like dying inside, for taking this blatantly honest approach, but it was a chance he was going to have to take. "They had the superior product. And you won't find anything on the market that rivals it. If they got some patents in place, you'd have a lock on the market with things like their lip gloss."

"Again, it wasn't about the product, it was about the deal." Now Mrs. Marion sounded annoyed, a bad sign. "I don't like wasting my time, Mark. I thought you'd know that by now. What do you want me to do?"

Mark took a deep breath. He felt as he had years ago, the first time he'd ever leaped off a high dive. And back then, he'd belly flopped nearly knocking himself unconscious.

Here's hoping this goes better.

"I think I've come up with a way to give the business to both Trimera and Diva Nation."

Mrs. Marion's expression, usually so carefully

schooled, now betrayed open shock. "How in the world do you think you'll manage that?" She laughed. "I don't know that you understand the point of an open competition for business, Mark!"

"First, if I could come up with a solution," Mark said doggedly, ignoring her obvious mocking, "would it be something you would be interested in? Something Marion & Co. would support?"

"Are you kidding? Those fabulous products, with the Trimera financial perks?" She was all but drooling over the possibility. Her grin was avaricious. "I would be more than interested, Mark. But I don't see how you'd pull it off."

Mark slowly outlined what he had in mind, and he saw the light of surprise turn to admiration in her eyes. "It won't be easy for me to convince my team," Mark finished, "but I think that it's the best solution for everyone."

Mrs. Marion smiled slowly. "What you're proposing goes far beyond a simple salesman's job," she said. "You're pulling off a big corporate deal, here. Does Trimera know what they have in you?"

Mark couldn't help it. He grinned. "I sure hope so."

"Although I will say, I wondered if your relationship with Sophie Jones would affect your business sense," she added, knocking his pride down dramatically. "If your company knows about your association with her…well, I imagine they wouldn't take it quite so favorably."

Mark set his jaw. He hadn't intended on discussing Sophie, or his relationship with her personally. "I suppose you've heard the rumors," he said, wondering how exactly to address it even as he resented the fact he was addressing it at all.

"Heard them?" Mrs. Marion laughed. "Dear boy, I started them."

Mark stared at her. "You did?"

"Well, Lily did," she amended. "She saw Ms. Jones going into your hotel room in San Francisco. I was somewhat surprised when Lily reported it to me, but I wasn't completely shocked. The chemistry between you two is rather obvious...if you're observant."

He got the feeling nothing made it past Mrs. Marion. "It didn't have any part in our competition," he pointed out, feeling like a broken record. How many times would he have to defend them?

If you do something stupid, you're going to have to pay the consequences.

"Obviously it didn't," Mrs. Marion agreed. "Otherwise, you never would have suggested knocking off her products. That power play impressed me, and really made me consider you and Trimera. Although I'm surprised Sophie didn't try to punch you right there!"

Mark winced. He hadn't been proud of that. The fact that Mrs. Marion was proud of his maneuver did nothing to improve the situation.

"But now—obviously you're feeling guilty," Mrs. Marion continued. "And that doesn't impress me, Mark. If you're servicing this account, I need to know that you'll be able to handle it. Emotions are wonderful things, and

I'm not saying you have to be an automaton. But business is business."

"This is business," Mark said firmly. "You want the best product for the best deal. Trimera wants the account, and Diva Nation needs the money. It's completely win-win."

"And Sophie has nothing to do with it?" she prompted.

Mark grimaced. "I won't try to lie and say she wasn't a factor," Mark said. "But if it weren't to our advantage, I wouldn't pursue it…even if it meant Diva Nation were out in the cold."

"Would she do the same thing, I wonder?"

"I'm sure she would," Mark said, even as he wondered about the statement. If she knew it would ruin his chances, would she be as business-minded? He wanted to say yes, but he wasn't sure. "She understands it's just business, and her family is important to her."

"Would you blame her, if the situation were reversed?"

"Of course not." Mark smiled, feeling more confident. He and Sophie had discussed that much, at least.

"You sound pretty sure of yourself." Mrs. Marion stood. "Well, then. Talk to your company, and I'll approach Diva Nation for one more meeting. It will be interesting to see how this all plays out."

"I'm sure it will work out beautifully," Mark said, shaking her hand.

"You know," Mrs. Marion said, "if Trimera doesn't go for it, maybe I could find a place for you here, in my organization. I'm always looking for talent that's hungry and creative." She winked. "And good-looking doesn't hurt."

She lingered in her handshake. It wasn't sexual, necessarily, but it did feel predatory. He knew how Mrs. Marion did business. He knew it could also be a possibly great opportunity. Nonetheless, he also knew that she wasn't the sort of person he wanted to work for directly.

"I appreciate the offer, Mrs. Marion," he said as politely as possible. "I'll have to see what happens."

"You do that," she said, still smiling.

Mark headed back to the Trimera office. Now, he had to make good on his promise…and make sure that everything turned out just the way he'd planned it.

"What are we doing here?" Sophie's mother whispered. "I thought we'd lost the account."

Sophie sat in a swanky restaurant in New York, at a large table. She hadn't revealed the details of her conversation with Mrs. Marion. She had hoped to convince the woman that Diva Nation was worth the effort, but she also knew that Mrs. Marion was, in a way, similar to her mother—more interested in cold, hard facts and scientific precision than touchy-feely issues. So Sophie had come up with a solution that would give her mother some breathing room, or so she thought. Mrs. Marion was intrigued. This, apparently, was the result.

She hadn't been able to talk to Mark, partially because she wasn't sure what to say. She wasn't trying to cut him out. She just couldn't leave her fate completely in his hands. It would put too much pressure on both of them. Besides, if this worked out, he'd probably still get the promotion, her mother would keep the house, and Sophie would be what she wanted to be more than anything in the world, these days. Completely free to make her own choices.

Please, please let this work!

"So many seats," her mother said, taking a nervous sip of her water. "Who are we expecting?"

"I don't know," Sophie admitted. "Mrs. Marion only told me to reserve a table for seven."

She wondered absently if Mrs. Marion would have the partnership papers with her. It was too soon, and Sophie knew that her mother was going to have to be slowly coaxed into the idea. But once she saw the numbers, Sophie felt sure that her mother would see that selling Diva Nation outright to Marion & Co. was the best and smartest option. It was just business.

She smirked bitterly. *Business was business.* At this rate, she could've sewn a needlepoint sampler that said the same. It was like her daily mantra.

Mrs. Marion walked up, Lily at her side as always. "It's so nice to see you again," she said in her smooth voice, sounding very pleased with herself. "I'm glad you agreed to meet with us."

"It's our pleasure," Sophie started, but her mother interrupted.

"It was our understanding that we lost the account,"

her mother said, and Sophie winced. "Has something changed?"

Mrs. Marion laughed. "Directness. I like that," she said easily. "Something has changed, indeed. I think we might be able to negotiate something beneficial after all."

Sophie felt her heart leap. Glancing at her mother, she saw both surprise and a renewed sense of hope. "I see," her mother said slowly.

"Unless you don't want the account?"

"Of course we want to work with you," Sophie assured her.

Mrs. Marion sat down. "I'm still expecting some people," she said, gesturing to the empty chairs, "but before they get here, I thought we'd lay out all the cards on the table. You like being direct—so do I."

Sophie felt some of her excitement ebb. Mrs. Marion looked stern.

"You're in financial trouble," Mrs. Marion said.

Sophie's mouth fell open. Her mother spluttered. "That's not relevant to these discussions—"

"Don't bother denying it," Mrs. Marion interrupted. "And it is relevant. I like to know who I'm working with. It was going to be enough of a problem dealing with a small company with vendor supply issues. But one on the brink of financial dissolution—well, that has *problem* written all over it."

Sophie felt the blood drain from her face. "We would be in the clear," she said, "if we got the Marion & Co. account."

"Barely," Mrs. Marion replied. "You'd still be struggling for that initial year, though. You need more than my account. You need an influx of capital, to keep yourselves going. And I don't want to work with a company that's struggling when it comes to something this prominent."

Sophie felt confused. Mrs. Marion was basically saying that there wasn't any way she'd work with Diva Nation…which wasn't what she'd said on the phone. What had changed between then and now?

"So why did you want to meet with us?" Sophie said, echoing her mother's question.

"Because I want to see if you understand the situation you're in," Mrs. Marion said sharply. "I decided to work with Trimera because they gave me concessions. You might not have the leverage—but you've got something I want. How badly do you want to get out of the hole you're in?"

Sophie turned to her mother, feeling flabbergasted. Of all the ways this meeting was going to run, she hadn't anticipated this turn of events at all. "Mom?" she asked softly. "It's your company. How badly do we want the account?"

Her mother's eyes lit with determination. "Mrs. Marion," she replied, her voice calm and proud, "I'll do almost anything to get this account. I believe in my company and our products. If you worked with us, I can promise that the results would be extraordinary."

"Ah, but what are you willing to give up?"

Sophie frowned. "What, exactly, are you asking for, Mrs. Marion?"

Before Mrs. Marion could answer, Sophie spied Mark, his boss Simone, and the man who had been present at the New York meeting—Roger, she believed his name was. They were making their way to the table. Sophie saw her mother tense and a look of hatred cross her face. "What are they doing here?" her mother demanded.

"This involves Trimera, as well," Mrs. Marion said mildly. "Mark, I'm glad you could make it."

Mark smiled at Sophie, and Sophie felt relief wash over her like a warm bath. He looked happy—confident. She noticed that Simone and Roger looked less happy. What had he pulled off?

She suddenly felt as if she'd been dumped into a frozen lake. She hadn't told him everything. Obviously, he'd been holding out on her, as well.

"Mrs. Jones," Mark said, holding his hand out to Sophie's mom cordially. She stared at it for a second, then shook it, disdain obvious on her face. She shot a quick glare at Sophie. "I suppose you're wondering what we're doing here."

"I haven't told them the deal," Mrs. Marion said, and damned if that amused grin of hers didn't pop back up. Sophie felt the creep of unease filter through her relief. "Since it was your idea, Mark, I thought I'd let you present it."

Sophie stared, totally shocked. *Mark's idea?*

"It's been patently obvious that Diva Nation's products were far better than anything Trimera had come up with," Mark said, earning a sour look from his boss. "And there was no way we could replicate the products with the same results. You *are* a cosmetics genius, Mrs. Jones."

Sophie's mom nodded in acceptance of the compliment. Sophie could tell she was a little mollified, even if she still didn't trust Mark.

"And I'm sure you realize that there's no way that your company could compete financially with Trimera," Mark continued. "That was how we won the account—with concessions and perks."

"That was the only way you could win," Sophie's mother interjected darkly.

"Mom," Sophie warned. "I'm sorry, Mark."

"So I proposed a compromise," Mark said. "Diva Nation's products, with Trimera's clout. The best of all possible worlds."

Sophie stared at him, unsure of where he was going.

"I'm not giving you the formulas," Sophie's mom said. "If you're going to knock them off, you'll have to figure it out yourselves."

"No, that's not what I'm saying at all," Mark said. "I still think that Diva Nation should create its own products. I think that the company should be partnered with Marion & Co, and continue with the work you've started."

Sophie blinked. "Maybe I'm just slow here," she said. "But what, exactly, are you proposing?"

Mark's smile was wide. "I'm saying that Trimera will purchase Diva Nation," he said. "Diva Nation will become a sub-brand, working with Marion & Co. We'll pay fair market value, don't worry, and we'll make sure that you're still involved with the running and operating of the company, since it's your innovation and creativity that's so valuable. We'll partner up. That way, Diva Nation becomes financially stable, Trimera gets a tremendous new brand, and Marion & Co. gets a great deal on a superior product. Everybody comes out ahead."

Sophie blinked, then almost burst out laughing. He'd thought the same thing she had—selling Diva Nation. *Great minds think alike,* she thought inanely.

"I figured you'd be up for it," Mrs. Marion said, "since you decided to try selling Diva Nation to me, Sophie."

Sophie's mother stared at her, as did Mark.

"So now, instead of Marion & Co. buying it, it'd be Trimera. Best of both possible worlds. What do you say?"

"It couldn't be more perfect," Sophie said softly to her mother. "What do you think?"

Her mother was silent for a long moment. Then she stood up.

"I think," she said coldly, "that you can all go to hell."

Sophie's eyebrows jumped up. "Mom?"

"Do you think I'm selling my company to the same jerks that fired me?" She grabbed up her purse, anger making her clumsy and catching the strap on the back of her chair. "Do you actually think I could trust you? Given the first opportunity, you'll drive Diva Nation right into the ground. No, thank you. I am not going to make this deal."

Mrs. Marion was frowning, as were Roger and Simone. Mark looked stunned.

"Excuse me," Sophie said. "I'll go talk to her." She followed her mother, almost running to catch up with her. "Mom, what are you doing?"

"The *nerve!*" her mother fumed. "The absolute *gall!*"

"But Mom, it solves everything," Sophie said, grabbing her mother's shoulder and forcing her to stop walking. "You'll be in the clear. You won't have to worry about money anymore. You'll keep the house—"

"I don't want to keep it that way," her mother said stubbornly.

Sophie felt like shaking her. "Damn it, I'm trying to help you here," she said. "I've done everything I can. Mark's gone above and beyond to help you. So why are you acting this way?"

Her mom's face was pensive. "I want to make sure I don't lose everything again," she said. "If only I could figure out some way to trust them, Sophie. You've been naive before. You think that this is perfect, and it looks it. The things that look perfect are the things that always wreck you in the end."

"So what do you want, Mom?" Sophie exploded, frustrated. "What would it take for you to trust them?"

Her mother sighed. "I don't know."

"Come back to the table," Sophie said.

Slowly, her mother went back with her. Roger and

Simone were talking to Mark, away from the table. Mrs. Marion was muttering something to Lily, who was taking down notes on her PDA. Mrs. Marion looked up.

"Is everything all right?" she asked mildly, but her expression was fierce.

Sophie's mom glanced at the Trimera contingent. "If this is going to go through," she said, "I'd want some assurances from you."

Mrs. Marion frowned. "I'll see what I can do."

"No, this would be a deal breaker," she responded.

Mrs. Marion stood. "Come walk with me," she said.

Sophie watched as her mother walked away with Mrs. Marion—something that Mark and his team also seemed to find disturbing. Mark sat next to Sophie. "What's going on?"

"I don't know," Sophie said. "But I think she's going to take the deal."

"She'd better," Mark said. "It's the only thing I could think of—and my neck's on the line now."

"We're all on the line," Sophie countered, and he nodded, breathing roughly.

"You can tell your mom when I'm in charge of the account, I'll make sure she doesn't get run into the ground," he said solemnly.

Sophie glanced over to where her mother was talking to Mrs. Marion in a low voice. "I'll try," she said.

But even as she promised, she now had the sinking feeling that, despite the solution, her mother wasn't going to take the easy way out.

11

"FOR GOD'S SAKE, MARK," Simone said with disgust, "after the conversation we had, I thought you were smarter than this."

Mrs. Marion had taken over, not surprisingly—and now he wasn't quite sure where the deal to purchase Diva Nation stood. Mark wasn't quite sure how he'd lost control of the situation.

He closed his eyes. No, he *did* know. He'd lost control when Sophie had entered the picture. And frankly, all hell had broken loose when her mother had decided to throw a wrench in the works.

"It should've been a straightforward deal," Mark muttered, taking a drink of his scotch and soda. "They should've jumped at it."

"You had the account. We didn't *need* them, damn it." Simone had a vodka martini in front of her. It was her second. Roger was off in a corner, muttering darkly on his cell phone. "You had the road to a big promotion in your grasp, and you decided to trash the whole damned thing. What were you thinking?"

"Hey," Mark said defensively, "buying Diva Nation

is a great step for Trimera. Roger thought so. So did his boss. If they didn't, we wouldn't have moved so fast on the offer."

Simone rolled her eyes. "Jesus, Mark, I know you have feelings for her, but I thought you had your head on straight. Now I can see that you're definitely making bad decisions because of that woman. And Roger— he's beyond angry."

"It's my account," Mark argued, feeling despondent. "He's pissed now, but give me a year. Once I show what I can do…"

"It won't matter," Simone informed him. "You jeopardized the team. It looks like you were showboating and you're trying to go over Roger's head. You can't possibly be that naive, to think that Roger's just interested in your performance. He's covering his own butt."

Mark winced. Yes, of course, he should know better. He hadn't meant to burn bridges. He'd hoped that Roger would see that this was a big step for everyone.

Apparently he'd gauged that one wrong, as well.

"You're lucky we still have the account, actually… and that Mrs. Marion likes you," Simone said. "Otherwise, I think that Roger would have you fired by the end of the day."

The statement sent a chill of dread over Mark. He gritted his teeth. "Well, we do still have the account, and all of this is going to work out," he finished grimly.

Simone did not look convinced.

Roger stalked back to the table. "They're going nuts

over at corporate," he said, glaring at Mark. "You and
your bright ideas. Why'd you get Mrs. Marion involved
in the first place? That woman's worse than a camel
trader. Whatever she's 'negotiating' with Diva Nation,
you know Trimera's going to get taken worse than it
already is. We gave her everything but the kitchen sink
to get her to choose us over them. And now we'll probably have to spend millions on a company that will be
a pain in the ass."

"I knew that if we approached Diva Nation separa-
tely, they might not listen," Mark replied, even though
he also felt that involving Mrs. Marion might've been
a mistake. "I knew that they saw the account as the one
thing that would save them. I figured bringing her in
would guarantee the sale."

"And look how well that turned out," Roger said sarcastically. "I'm sorry we went after the damned account
in the first place!"

"I'm sorry to hear that," a woman's voice intoned.

Mark turned to see Mrs. Marion standing by their
table. He winced. Roger at least looked embarrassed.
Simone didn't change expression; she simply downed
the rest of her martini and motioned to the waiter for a
refill. Meanwhile, Sophie and her mother seemed to
have left the restaurant.

Mark stared at Mrs. Marion, whose face was solemn—
and he got the feeling that, whatever she was about to
announce, it wasn't good.

"You can cheer up," she said. "The deal is going

through. Mrs. Jones and your CEO just settled on a price, and lawyers will be drawing up paperwork in the next few weeks."

Mark felt his body relax, a smile crossing his face. "You're a miracle worker," he said. He knew that Roger would still be angry, and Simone disappointed, but at least he'd gotten what he set out for. Sophie must feel even more relieved. He couldn't wait to hear what Sophie had to say.

"But there were some additional provisions," she said. "Mrs. Jones was quite adamant about that."

Mark blanched. He should have known. Still, it was better than nothing. "What sort of provisions?"

She shook her head. "The thing she was most afraid of was that Trimera's marketing department would try and alter the course of her company—change her products, change their packaging, what have you. She doesn't trust the management."

"Well, we did fire her," Mark said. "I'll do what I can to reassure her. I'm sure I can put something in writing, incorporate it in the sale paperwork…"

"You don't understand," Mrs. Marion said. "The only way she'd sell was to ensure that they'd stay true to their original vision. She's insisting on choosing her own account manager."

Mark felt his blood run cold. "But I'm the account manager."

"Not anymore." Mrs. Marion shrugged. "She's insisted on having her daughter Sophie take over that role. The sale was contingent on that issue."

"And…Sophie's taking the job?" Mark asked.

Mrs. Marion nodded. "I'm sorry. But you were right, Mark. This deal is the best for everyone." She paused. "Well, it was the best for my company, anyway. I'm glad you brought it up." Another pause. "And good luck."

With that, she turned and left.

Mark downed the rest of his drink. "Waiter," he said, pointing to his empty glass.

Roger rubbed at his temples with his fingertips. "Well, if that's not ironic."

"Still glad you slept with her?" Simone asked.

That was when Mark realized—Simone had been covering her own ass. As much as she'd supported him, the moment she realized he was going to be promoted to her level, she'd taken steps to ensure her own longevity.

He'd gotten screwed in more ways than one.

"So you're not going to be the account person," Roger said slowly.

Mark waited for him to finish the statement. Roger looked at him intently, as Simone continued drinking.

"I'm fired, aren't I?" Mark finally supplied.

Roger nodded. "You'll get the official word on Monday," he said. "And a package."

Mark didn't hear the rest of what Roger had to say. He politely excused himself and exited the place as fast as his legs could carry him.

In one short day, trying to help the woman he loved, he'd lost the prize account, his promotion…his *job*. His future was in shambles.

He had to talk to Sophie. He had planned to meet her at her hotel later that night anyway. Change of plans. It only took him fifteen minutes to reach her door. He knocked, conflicting emotions swirling through him chaotically.

She opened the door. "I didn't know until we'd left the restaurant," she said by way of greeting.

"I got fired," he said, walking in. The shock still reverberated through him.

"Oh, God, I'm so sorry," she said, hugging him. "I didn't know this was going to work out this way."

"I did all this trying to help you," he said. "I thought I had it all planned."

"I can't thank you enough," Sophie breathed, kissing his neck, his chin. "Now, my mom's retirement is secure, and her house…"

"I won't get my promotion," he pointed out. "Hell, I don't even know where I'll get another job, Sophie!"

"I'm sorry," she repeated. Then, slowly, she offered, "I could get you a job in the department. I mean, I am account manager."

He stared at her. "You *took my job,* Sophie."

Sophie blushed. "It was the only way my mom would sell," she said slowly. "I'm sorry, but…Mark, I couldn't do that to her again."

He closed his eyes. "And that's it, huh?"

"You felt that way when you won the account," she pleaded. "I was out of a job, and I still wanted to be with you…."

"I put everything on the line to help you!"

Her eyes were wide and rimmed with tears. "I can't jeopardize her again," Sophie said. "The best I can do is get you a job working for me. You'll still have a career…."

"When everybody knows we slept together?" he asked, feeling despair wash over him. "Sophie, I've spent my whole life trying to prove I got where I am because of my own merits. Not because of my face. Not because I slept my way to the top!" He felt like hurling something against the wall. "So now I've got nothing!"

"I don't know how to help you," Sophie said.

"I don't know how, either," Mark said.

"Where does that leave us?" Sophie said as he turned and headed for the door.

Mark paused. He still wanted Sophie. But wanting her had gotten him here, in this position. Nothing had been clear or right since then.

"I need to figure things out," Mark said. "When I do…I'll get in contact with you. Okay?"

"And that's it?" Sophie said.

"For now," Mark said. "Yeah. That's it."

Sophie nodded, tears spilling down her cheeks. "And if you don't figure things out?" she whispered. "Or…you figure out that we were a mistake?"

Mark didn't know what to say. So he didn't say anything. Instead, he left.

"YOU'VE BEEN AWFULLY QUIET."

Mark was watching the sun set from his parents'

porch in Knoxville. He turned to look at his brother Jeff, standing framed in the front doorway. "Just relaxing."

"It's been great to have you down," Jeff said. "The kids love visiting with Uncle Mark."

Mark felt a stab of guilt. "I'm sorry I haven't gotten down here more often, Jeff."

"We know how important your job was to you," Jeff said, compounding the problem. "And I'm really sorry about what happened."

Mark nodded. Of course, he hadn't gone into the full, ugly details of what had happened. They knew that he'd lost his job, but to their credit, they hadn't pried. His family had welcomed him as always, with open arms.

After his troubles with Trimera, it was a reassuring balm. If only his troubles with Sophie could be soothed away as easily.

Jeff sat down on the other bench, looking at him intently. "So what will you do next?"

"I'm not sure." Mark picked up his glass of iced tea. "Get another job, obviously."

"Yeah," Jeff said. "Keeping that fancy place in New York can't be cheap."

Mark grimaced. "Don't put it that way. You and Margo and the kids have a great house, you know."

"I'm not judging," Jeff replied. "And yes, we do have a great house. I earn a good living. But…" He let the sentence peter off, frowning.

Mark glanced at him. "Just spit it out."

"Mom and Dad won't bring it up, they're just glad

to see you," Jeff said thoughtfully. "But they're thinking it, all the same."

"Thinking *what?*"

"Ever since you were a model, things went a little screwy for you."

Mark groaned. "Jeez, we're going to go *that* far back? I know nobody liked the idea of me modeling. I know a lot of people around here thought that it wasn't a man's job. And then getting a job with a cosmetics company…"

"Mom and Dad didn't give a damn about that, and you know it," Jeff scoffed. "It was when you started making a lot of money. People were treating you differently. You went to New York, and you lost your head. Suddenly you had something to prove. You were successful as a model because of your looks, so suddenly you had to show everybody how smart you are. You were successful as a salesman because you're friendly, and suddenly you've got to show everybody that you can be a cutthroat businessman, just like anybody else." Jeff shook his head. "Honestly, you've been the biggest jackass for the past few years, but you haven't been around enough for me to get the chance to tell you so. So now I am."

Mark stared at his brother, shocked. "I thought you were proud of how I was doing at my job!"

Jeff laughed. "Damn, Mark, we all knew you were smart before you left. The fact that people thought you were just a pretty boy was funny. But you seemed to buy into it. It's like you forgot how smart you were."

Mark stood up and started pacing, feeling embarrassment start to course through him.

"Next thing I knew, you were telling me about how many hours you were working and all of your travel," Jeff continued relentlessly. "You never talked about anybody else."

"I dated," Mark protested…until he saw Jeff's knowing smirk. "Okay. So I didn't have a lot of time for a relationship."

"You didn't have a lot of time for anything," Jeff said. "Now, you'll have plenty of time. My question is—are you dumb enough to jump right back on that treadmill, or will you begin figuring out what's really important in your life?"

Mark felt like an idiot. "What if I told you I have started seeing someone?"

Jeff grinned broadly. "I'd say it's about time, and why isn't she here?"

"We sort of had a falling out."

"Already?" Jeff shook his head. "What happened?"

"It sort of had to do with my job."

"Ah. You put your job before your relationship with her, I'll bet," Jeff said sagely.

"No." Then Mark thought about it…about all the conversations they'd had, about keeping business and personal separate. "Well, maybe. But it was more like she put her job before me."

"No kidding." Jeff rubbed at his jaw thoughtfully. "What happened?"

In bits and pieces, Mark relayed the whole ugly scenario to him. He'd always been able to talk to Jeff, and now that the story was off his chest, he wondered why he hadn't talked to his family sooner. He felt better—still hurting from the loss, but a little more comfortable with it.

"Now let me get this straight," Jeff said. "She took your job?"

"Yes."

"Because her mom's retirement depended on it?"

Mark frowned. "It didn't…at least, not at first. Her mom pulled a power play and made it necessary for Sophie to take the job, or she'd walk away from the sale. See, I said it was complicated."

"No, it isn't," Jeff protested. "Was it Sophie's idea to take your job?"

"Well, no."

"And if she didn't take the job, her mom would've walked and then lost her house and all her money, right?"

"It was her own choice, though—"

"Boy, I take back what I said. Nobody smart would say something like that." Jeff crossed his arms. "I'm not saying the mom was right for doing what she did, but you can't blame that girl for taking the job and standing up for her family. Sounds like she did the right thing, and she wanted you to understand. But you let the whole thing get all twisted, and then you walked away."

"It's not that easy."

"It's not easy," Jeff said. "But do you love her?"

Mark had been twisted in knots over that very question since the day he'd been fired. Longer than that, if he thought about it. "I love her," he said. "But…"

"No buts," Jeff countered. "If you love her, then this is a problem, but it's not the end of it. You need to talk this out with her."

"I need to get my career in place first," Mark said sharply.

"Mark, there are more important things than a career," Jeff said.

"I know that!" Mark didn't mean to yell and was surprised to hear his own voice sounding so sharp. "You think I don't know that? This isn't just about the job, though. You said that you knew I was smart. Well…I guess I didn't. I wasn't trying to prove something to those jerks over in New York. I wasn't even trying to prove something to the woman I love. I was trying to prove something to *me,* that I could make it on my own. Not because of my looks, but because of who I was."

Jeff was quiet for a long moment. "I'm sorry," he said, and his voice sounded sincere. "I really didn't know you felt that way."

"Yeah, well, you were always the smart one," Mark said, knowing that it was true. "And Mom and Dad were good businesspeople. And there I was, making money by getting my picture taken, and everybody thought it was a big joke. Thought *I* was a big joke."

"Does this woman love you?"

"She says she does," Mark said. "No. I'm sure she

does. And maybe it's dumb to need to prove myself. But if I don't do this…I'll always wonder, and it'll always stand between us."

His brother clapped a hand on his shoulder. "Do what you have to do, Mark," Jeff said. "But I will say this— don't wait forever to figure this out. Don't wait until you make your first million. Otherwise, you're going to find out that as proud as you are of yourself, she's moved on while you were out proving yourself."

Mark felt a cold chill wash over him. "I'm praying it doesn't get to that point," he said vehemently.

Jeff sighed. "I'll pray for both of you."

12

"SOPHIE," HER MOTHER SAID, when she opened the door of her mom's home. "You look terrible!"

"Hi to you, too, Mom," Sophie said, putting her laptop case and purse on the kitchen table.

Her mother reddened. "I'm sorry. It's that…I haven't seen you in a few months." She bit her lip. "You've lost weight."

"I've been busy," Sophie said.

"I know," her mother said, and her voice was shaded with tones of pride. "I've been reading about Diva Nation in the trade mags, and when I saw the display they put out in the Marion & Co. over in Santa Monica—oh, Sophie, it was everything I could've dreamed of. And then some."

"You've got Lydia to thank for that," Sophie said. "The launch went better than we'd hoped. Orders are pouring in. You should have your retirement covered, and then some."

"And how is working with Trimera?" her mother asked eagerly. "I'll bet they're choking on it, having to work with you."

"Some of them are," Sophie admitted, "but only because they worked so hard internally, and they didn't want to see somebody on the outside taking over and messing stuff up. I showed them I knew what I was doing, we figured out how to work together. Problem solved, drama over."

Her mother blinked. "You sound angry."

"I'm tired," Sophie said. Then she sat down. "No, you're right. I'm angry."

"What did they do?" her mother said, sitting down, her face concerned.

"It's not what they did," Sophie said. "It's what you did."

"What I did?" Her mother sighed. "Sophie, you knew what this meant to me. You knew…"

"I knew what it meant to you," Sophie replied. "Did it ever occur to you what this would mean to me?"

Her mother was quiet for a long moment. "Is this about that man again?"

Sophie winced. Just thinking about Mark…it had been six long months, and she hadn't heard from him. Hadn't even heard *of* him. Apparently, he'd disappeared from the cosmetics industry altogether. "This isn't about him," Sophie continued. "That's over, anyway. I don't even know where he is."

"I said I was sorry about that," her mother said defensively.

"I know. But your company was more important."

Her mother sat up straighter in her chair. "All my

future and my finances were tied up in it," she said. "I suppose you wanted me to be a bag lady?"

"Here's the thing," Sophie said. "You didn't have to be. You could have sold Diva Nation without any stipulations, and still been set for life. But you had to make sure that I was running it."

"I had to make sure that they didn't drive the company that I'd created into the ground with crappy products and stupid management decisions," she replied. "I had to make sure that it was in the hands of someone I trusted!"

"No, actually, you didn't," Sophie said. "And the worst part is, I let you. I knew that you'd be stubborn enough to sabotage your own welfare out of spite."

"You make me sound like a six-year-old."

"You've been acting like one," Sophie said. "I love you, Mom. But this has got to stop."

Her mother stood up and started pacing. "Is this the conversation we have, where I'm Mommy Dearest, and I don't let you—"

"I've got an ulcer, Mom."

Her mother stopped cold. "What? When did you find out about this?"

"I've been working my butt off, trying to make Diva Nation everything you wanted it to be," Sophie said. "I was working ninety-hour weeks. I didn't have Mark in my life or anybody else."

"You can't blame that on me," her mother said, obviously sounding shaken.

"I don't," Sophie said. "I blame that on me. I was

working too hard and for the wrong reasons." She took a deep breath. "Diva Nation is doing fine. I've got a team in place that will make sure it continues producing the quality products we're known for. And now that it's on its way…I'm quitting. I wanted to tell you myself, before I announced anything official."

Her mother continued pacing. "You shouldn't have worked so hard," she chided.

Sophie smiled gently. "I know. I've been trying to prove myself to you, and trying to do what I keep thinking you want. That's dumb."

"I never…" Her mother couldn't even continue the sentence. "I didn't do this to you," she repeated.

"No. I did this to me," Sophie said, getting up and standing next to her mother. "And now I'm not going to do that anymore."

She hugged her mother, and to her surprise, her mother started to cry.

"I know…I know I put you in a bad position," she said against Sophie's shoulder. "I just wanted to get even with those bastards so badly! They ruined me. I wasn't going to let them win."

"So you kept control," Sophie said.

"And you paid for it." Her mother took a deep breath. "I made my point, and you made yours. I'm sorry for that." She paused. "So you'll walk away from it, then?"

"Yes."

"There's no way you could maybe take a break, and go back?"

Sophie stared at her mother, then shook her head. "I'm done," she said softly. "I want to get my own job and live my own life from now on."

Her mother frowned, but nodded. "I can understand that."

They stood there for a moment, silently taking the situation in. Then her mother wiped at her eyes and stepped away.

"Do you know what you're going to be doing?"

"I don't know," Sophie admitted. It had been freeing enough just to think of quitting Diva Nation. She hadn't formulated a plan from that point. "Finding a job, I imagine. Something else in the cosmetics industry…or maybe not. I don't know."

"You might want to take a break," her mother suggested. "With that ulcer, and all."

Sophie gave a short laugh. "I can buy a little time…a few months. But then, back to work."

"You know, if it weren't for your strategy and planning, and hard work, I never would've been able to sell Diva Nation for as much as I did," her mother said. "I want to give you some of the money from the sale."

Sophie shook her head. "That's for your retirement."

"I bled them dry," her mother said with a snort. "I made out better than I could've dreamed, and you know it. I've got plenty left over. You'll take some of it, and I don't want to hear any arguments." She smiled weakly. "Let me pay off some of this guilt."

Sophie sighed. "All right, Mom. You win."

"So maybe you'll take a vacation," her mother said. "Maybe…start dating."

It was a big concession for her take-no-prisoners, business-is-everything mother. Sophie thought it was a good step forward. Still, the thought of dating made her chest ache. She didn't want to date. She didn't want to find someone.

She'd already found Mark, and then she'd lost him. That was painful enough.

"I'll just take a break," Sophie said. "Rest up."

"It will get better," her mother whispered.

Sophie nodded. "I know," she said, even though she only knew it logically. Emotionally, she still felt like a wreck.

"So, have you already given notice?"

Sophie nodded. "I'll be making the management-changeover announcement at the sales conference in San Antonio." One year ago, she thought. At the same conference she'd met Mark.

"I'm sure it'll be a big event," her mother said.

"It will be memorable," Sophie said. She certainly wouldn't forget it.

"MARK MCMANN?"

Mark stood up, feeling acutely self-conscious. He wore a suit, but he appeared to be the only guy in the building to do so, and he felt a bit like a circus freak. He'd only seen one woman, who was wearing sweats, her hair in a ponytail. She had smiled at him. Everybody else there was a guy, all wearing jeans or khakis and T-shirts that sported various humorous slogans or TV-show pictures. There was a lot of *Star Trek* present, he noticed.

He followed the guy who seemed to be acting as receptionist and jack-of-all-trades into the main "office" of the man he was interviewing with.

"Mark! Good to see you!" The chief executive officer, Frank Stone, was wearing a pair of black jeans and a Sealab 2021 T-shirt. He also gave Mark's suit a curious glance as he shook his hand. "Glad you could make it all the way out here to California to see us."

"Looked forward to it," Mark said, and he meant it.

"So. I've been reviewing your résumé. I have to say—it's nothing like anybody else's that has applied for the job here at Game Preserve."

Mark had expected not—considering his entire background was in beauty and cosmetics, and this was a new video-game start-up. "Well, it wouldn't seem like it would translate, but I've got a lot of national distribution and brand experience."

"I can see that," Frank said, and Mark felt gratified at the appreciative tone in the guy's voice. "But tell me… we're not going to be able to pay you as much as your old company did. Why do you want to work for us?"

Mark thought about everything that had happened in the past twelve months. Meeting Sophie. Falling in love with Sophie. Losing Sophie. Losing the job at Trimera because of Sophie. In roughly that order.

"I need a change," Mark said, thinking *understate-*

ment of the year. "I used to love video games as a kid and I've rediscovered them since then. Meanwhile, I've learned everything I needed to at my old job, and now I'm looking for a challenge."

"Well, we'll definitely be that," Frank said.

The two of them talked shop for a while, and by the end of the interview, Mark felt as if he'd done the best he could—laid out what he thought Game Preserve's strategy should be, the whole nine yards. Now, it was in their hands.

Frank stood up, stretching, and Mark assumed that the interview was over, so he stood up, too, offering his hand again. But Frank laughed.

"No, I'll be taking you out to lunch, too, if you're up for it. I won't beat around the bush. I like you, and even though your background is completely wrong for us, I go with my gut on this sort of thing. But you'll have to run the gamut if you're going to work here."

Mark straightened up. "I have no problem with that. I'm just looking for a chance."

Frank's eyes glinted, and Mark suddenly wondered what the hell he had agreed to. Frank opened his office door, motioning for Mark to follow. "Okay, guys!" Frank yelled down the corridor. "We've got a candidate!"

With that, a wide range of men came pouring out of cubicles and headed for a large lounge-looking area. Mark swallowed nervously, wondering if this was some sort of arcane ritual akin to hazing. And he'd thought that the cosmetics industry was rough.

They were staring at him like a sacrificial lamb, and Mark refused to blink.

"Okay," Frank said, crossing his arms. "Five minutes. Let 'im have it."

Before Mark could react to that sweeping statement, he was peppered with questions.

"Where do you buy most of your video games?"

"What's the best game you've bought in the past year?"

"What do you own?"

His head spun as the voices came yelling out at him, like a squalling mob. He took a deep breath. "Y'all done?" he asked easily.

They went quiet, expectant.

One more deep breath, and then he marked everyone who'd asked him a question. "I get my games anywhere I'm in town, usually at a game store because the clerks know what I'm talking about, sometimes online if I have the time," he said to a stocky guy with thick glasses. "I own an Xbox, a PS2, a Game Boy, my PDA's equipped, and I've got some stuff on my PC at home," he said to a thin, tall Asian man, who grinned in response. "And the best game I've bought in the past year is Halo 2…and I'd challenge anybody in here to try and take me on it, after the hours I've logged."

"We'll take you up on that!" a short kid with a backward baseball cap said, and the rest of them laughed.

Mark let out a quick huff. He'd survived the lion's den. Frank looked puffed up with pride.

"Why don't we go to lunch," he said with a broad grin, "and discuss some particulars. Like salary, and benefits."

Mark nodded to the assorted guys, who nodded back in return. "Welcome to the team," the Asian guy said with a smile.

Mark felt his spine straighten. Part of the team. One of the guys.

Sophie had believed in him…and here he was, striking out on his own. This wasn't about his looks, or his charm. This was finally what it meant to make it on his own, on his brains and his abilities.

He smiled as he followed Frank out the door, onto the street.

As he'd told his brother, he just wanted to prove to himself that he could handle it. It had taken longer than he'd thought to find a situation that suited him—six months of searching, and getting rid of his stuff in New York, simplifying his life. He'd briefly taken a job at Marion & Co., insisting that he not work on anything related to Diva Nation, but even that near proximity had been too much. Besides that—Mrs. Marion had shown him how he didn't want to do business.

"I thought you had better business instincts than that, Mark," she'd said when he'd finally given in and quit.

He'd made the right choice. He didn't know how Sophie was managing, caught between the Scylla and Charybdis of Marion & Co. and Trimera. But from everything he'd been able to find out, things were going spectacularly well for her. Diva Nation was splashed across the pages of every trade magazine he read, and all of his contacts said that Trimera was set to make millions upon millions thanks to their investment in the boutique company. It looked like Mark's instincts had been dead-on, after all. And Sophie was the brains behind the success. He imagined that must have bothered Simone, who'd taken a job with one of their competitors not long after. Roger had been promoted as a result, so he had to be happy.

Mark wondered if Sophie was happy.

"So now that your life's in order," his brother said, when Mark called to tell him the good news, "what are you going to do about the girl?"

Mark wondered about that, too. "It's been a long while. I'm sure she's moved on."

"In other words, you're chickening out."

"I am not chickening out," Mark snapped. "I…she's probably really ticked at me for not calling, even if she is interested, which she probably isn't."

"You're the one who had to figure stuff out," Jeff said. "I get the feeling she'll understand. And even if she doesn't…"

"I know. I have to try." Mark chuckled bitterly. "Man. I've done sales pitches and job interviews and multimillion-dollar deals, and just calling her has me more nervous than anything I've ever done."

"Maybe you should see her face-to-face," Jeff suggested. "You're always better in person, if I remember correctly."

Mark thought about it. "The trade mags did say she had some big announcement or something at the next conference."

"Where's that?"

Mark consulted the magazine he had on his coffee table, then grinned slowly. "Well, I'll be damned. San Antonio."

"Sounds like you've been there."

Mark grinned. "We've both been there," he said. "And I think that luck is finally going my way."

SOPHIE SAT IN HER HOTEL ROOM in San Antonio, looking out into the night sky. She felt free, and curiously empty. She could still remember every word she'd spoken at the press conference in the main ballroom that afternoon.

"I would like to thank Marion & Co. for the wonderful opportunity they presented by choosing the Diva Nation line of cosmetics as their house brand," she'd opened. "I would also like to thank Trimera for the exciting working partnership they offered. I know that the companies will work beautifully together in years to come. I also would like to thank everyone involved for their support. From now on, I know that Diva Nation is in good hands. That's why I'm taking this opportunity to step down from my position as director of marketing and sales for Diva Nation."

There had been some shock over that, but all in all, they weren't interested in her. They were interested in the products. Sophie could go back to her own life now, such as it was. That was, she could actually *have* a life now.

She was looking forward to the chance.

It would have been nice to share this moment with someone, she realized absently as she sipped at a diet soda and put her feet up on the bed. Her mother and sister had volunteered to accompany her, but she'd turned them down. Lydia was now busy with her own graphic-design firm thanks to the exposure she got from designing the packaging and ads for Diva Nation's launch. Her mother, on the other hand, was finally letting things go and settling into retirement. After years of working and struggling, relaxation was coming hard to her, but Sophie had to be thankful she was trying. Sophie didn't want to ruin that progress by putting her in close proximity with Trimera execs again. So here she was, alone at what was definitely a huge turning point in her life.

I wonder what Mark's doing.

She wondered that at least ten times a day, so she wasn't surprised when the thought appeared, unbidden. Now she had time for a social life, one that included dating—and sex. There wouldn't be business between them anymore, she thought. Still, she didn't know if there were still hard feelings on his part.

You knew it wouldn't be simple, she reminded herself for the billionth time. She had thought that they could manage, and for a while they had, but inevitably it had blown up in their faces.

The question was…was the damage irreparable?

She closed her eyes. She now had money to breathe, to take time off. She would have energy, once she'd slept for about a week. She still wasn't quite sure what had imploded with Mark, to cause him to cut off all contact. Part of her was still angry at the course he'd taken. Part of her was furious that he hadn't even tried to contact her once. But a big part of her still loved him, and missed him. That part was willing to invest the time and energy to find him, and try to get back what they'd lost. The worst that could happen would be him saying no, and turning away from her. She hadn't come this far in her business by letting every *No* stand in her way, she thought with a tired smile.

There was a knock on her door. She didn't want to deal with a restaurant full of industry insiders, so she'd ordered room service. She got the door and her mouth fell open.

"This steak for you?"

It was Mark, standing there with the room-service cart. He wasn't the polished, business Mark that she was used to seeing. He was wearing a T-shirt and jeans, and looked scruffy, casual and utterly delicious. She nodded dumbly, watching as he rolled in her dinner. She let the door shut. "I can't believe you're here," she finally said. "I was just thinking about you."

He grinned, the same sweet, irrepressible grin she remembered. Her heart tugged in response. "I always think about you," he replied.

She crossed her arms. *Don't let him in that easily.* "You could have fooled me," she said lightly, "considering I haven't heard from you since that day in New York. Six months ago."

He kept his eyes on her, sitting on the bed. "I am sorry about that. I needed to get my head on right, sort out what I was doing with my life."

"And you couldn't have told me that?" She felt tears start to well up in her eyes, and she blinked hard to prevent them. She just wanted the air clear. She wasn't about to lose her composure and be reduced to jelly at his feet…at least, not before they'd talked.

"I didn't know how to tell you," he said, and his tone sounded miserable. "I was angry with you initially. Really, I was more angry with myself. I felt like a failure. I thought everybody around me saw me as a failure, and I wasn't bouncing back from that."

"*I* didn't think you were a failure," Sophie pointed out.

He stood up, moved next to her, and his arms reached for her tentatively, stroking her shoulders. The instinct was great to let him fold her into his arms, but she held back, keeping her gaze intent on his. "I know," he finally said. "You always believed in me. But until I believed in myself, you couldn't believe in me enough for both of us. Does that make sense?"

"No," she said, her voice trembling slightly.

"I needed to prove something to myself," he said. "I wanted to know I could make it on my own."

"You would have made it on your own," she answered. "But you didn't have to be alone. I would've been supportive."

"I know that now," he said. "Believe me, for someone who was trying to prove how smart he was, I can be amazingly stupid."

She laughed. She couldn't help it. He smiled, and she felt her defenses start to crumble.

"Now I know I can make it on my own…but I don't want to," he pleaded. "I don't want to spend any more time away from you. I just got a job, one I really like, in San Diego. I know you're in Los Angeles. I don't mind commuting."

"Haven't you heard? I'm currently between jobs," she said. "So I don't have to stay in L.A." In fact, she realized, it might be good to put some distance between her and her family. For that matter, it'd be good to start fresh in a new city. The thought made her smile more.

"I saw the press conference," he said, stroking her arms. She gave in, leaning toward him. He hugged her tightly. "I know how hard you worked. Everyone knows that the success was thanks to you and they're all dying to snap you up. You could name your price and your terms. You can get anything you want."

"Right now, all I want is you."

She hadn't meant to say that. Not yet. But his hug turned fierce, and he leaned down, kissing her with abandon. She gave in, hunger driving her to run her fingers through his hair and kiss him as though she hadn't in a hundred years. That was certainly what it felt like. The familiar feel of him made yearning shoot through her like nothing else.

"Can you forgive me?" he said after tearing himself away. He kissed her jaw, her throat, the sweet spot behind her earlobe. "Can we fix everything?"

"I forgave you the minute you walked in with my dinner," she said with a shaky laugh, and his answering chuckle warmed her right down to her toes. "I know. I shouldn't make it that easy on you, but I love you. And I've missed you. I thought you'd broken my heart."

"I will spend the rest of my life," he said solemnly, all humor erased from his voice, "making it up to you."

"You'd better." She felt heat start to seep through her, starting in her chest and radiating out. "In fact, starting now would be perfect."

His wicked smile of response was enough to set her nerve endings tingling. "What about your dinner?" he asked, his tone mock innocent.

"What dinner?"

He laughed out loud. "Well, I can think of something more appealing."

With that, he tugged her over to the bed. Her fingers flew to the buttons on her blouse as he tugged off his T-shirt and shucked his jeans and boxers. She tore her sleeve in her haste, causing him to laugh again. By the time she stripped out of her skirt and underwear, all laughter had ceased. They stared at each other for a moment.

"I didn't think I'd ever get the chance to do this again," she breathed.

"It feels like the first time," he said. Then slowly,

reverently, he reached for her, softly caressing her shoulder, smoothing his fingertips down her side and hip, reaching between her legs and touching ever so gently between her curls. She gasped, her hips arching for more intimate contact. His eyes went dark with passion. She grabbed one of the condoms he'd tossed on the bed when he'd taken off his jeans. After ripping it open with shaking hands, she smoothed it on slowly over his rock-hard erection, the heat of him warming her palm as she rolled it. He groaned, his hips bucking in response. They inched slowly next to each other, warming each other with the slide of naked skin over naked skin. It did feel like the first time, she marveled. He kissed her collarbone as she rubbed her breasts over his chest, feeling his cock poke against her belly. Her leg trailed over his, her thighs heating and her flesh going damp with desire. She reached down and positioned him between her legs, her breathing going uneven. He cupped one breast as his hips angled slightly, dipping himself into her. She gasped slightly, from the overwhelming sensation of his fingers on her nipple and his cock penetrating her slowly. "Mark," she said, her last coherent thought before pleasure slammed through her, rendering her giddy.

He nudged her from her side onto her back, the action causing more of him to slide into her, stretching her out, filling her. She arched her hips, feeling the pressure of him as his hips slid between her thighs. She wanted more—she wanted all of him. He slowly buried himself all the way inside her, and he was familiar and yet so unfamiliar after all this time that it was like reliving a dream. She moaned as he withdrew by centimeters, the friction of him against her clit slowly driving her mad.

"I want you," she whispered.

"I won't rush this," he replied through gritted teeth. "I'm going to make you crazy with it. I've been dreaming of this so often…."

"So have I…*oh*," she interrupted herself, as he pressed back inside her. His fingers reached down, finding her sensitive spot and circling it with his thumb. Before she even realized what was happening, her breathing sped up and she climaxed, a short, sharp swirl of sensation. *"Mark!"*

When she focused on his face, he was smiling with satisfaction, even as there was a sheen of sweat across his forehead. His hips moved in timeless rhythm, and she shifted her own hips to match him perfectly. She had one more orgasm roar through her. "Mark," she pleaded. "Please…"

Finally, as if he could no longer hold back, his timing quickened, and his breathing went shallow and more hoarse. She felt the bunching of his muscles in his back and hips, and she touched them gently, wrapping her legs around his waist and holding on tight. She couldn't believe it when she felt the unmistakable signs of yet another orgasm starting to creep up on her, and she shouted when it finally hit, feeling him shuddering against her as he finally allowed himself release.

When it was over, she kissed him, long and deep. "Don't ever leave me again," she said firmly.

He smiled down at her. "I won't," he promised. "And I won't let something stupid like business get between us again."

"So...I guess this is going to be longer than just one night," she said with a quicksilver grin.

"Lady," he answered with a wink, "if it was, this night's going to last forever."

* * * * *

THE ROYAL HOUSE OF NIROLI
Always passionate, always proud

The richest royal family in the world—united
by blood and passion, torn apart by deceit and desire

Nestled in the azure blue of the Mediterranean Sea, the
majestic island of Niroli has prospered for centuries.
The Fierezza men have worn the crown with passion
and pride since ancient times. But now, as the king's
health declines, and his two sons have been tragically
killed, the crown is in jeopardy.

The clock is ticking—a new heir must be found before the king is forced to abdicate. By royal decree the
internationally scattered members of the Fierezza
family are summoned to claim their destiny. But any
person who takes the throne must do so according to
The Rules of the Royal House of Niroli. Soon secrets
and rivalries emerge as the descendants of this ancient
royal line vie for position and power. Only a true
Fierezza can become ruler—a person dedicated to their
country, their people…and their eternal love!

*Each month starting in July 2007, Harlequin Presents
is delighted to bring you an exciting installment from*
THE ROYAL HOUSE OF NIROLI,
*in which you can follow the epic search
for the true Nirolian king.
Eight heirs, eight romances, eight fantastic stories!*

Here's your chance to enjoy a sneak preview of the
first book delivered to you by royal decree…

FIVE minutes later she was standing immobile in front of the study's window, her original purpose of coming in forgotten, as she stared in shocked horror at the envelope she was holding. Waves of heat followed by icy chill surged through her body. She could hardly see the address now through her blurred vision, but the crest on its left-hand front corner stood out, its *royal* crest, followed by the address: *HRH Prince Marco of Niroli...*

She didn't hear Marco's key in the apartment door, she didn't even hear him calling out her name. Her shock was so great that nothing could penetrate it. It encased her in a kind of bubble, which only concentrated the torment of what she was suffering and branded it on her brain so that it could never be forgotten. It was only finally pierced by the sudden opening of the study door as Marco walked in.

"Welcome home, *Your Highness*. I suppose I ought to curtsy." She waited, praying that he would laugh and tell her that she had got it all wrong, that the envelope she was holding, addressing him as Prince Marco of

Niroli, was some silly mistake. But like a tiny candle flame shivering vulnerably in the dark, her hope trembled fearfully. And then the look in Marco's eyes extinguished it as cruelly as a hand placed callously over a dying person's face to stem their last breath.

"Give that to me," he demanded, taking the envelope from her.

"It's too late, Marco," Emily told him brokenly. "I know the truth now…." She dug her teeth in her lower lip to try to force back her own pain.

"You had no right to go through my desk," Marco shot back at her furiously, full of loathing at being caught off guard and forced into a position in which he was in the wrong, making him determined to find something he could accuse Emily of. "I trusted you…."

Emily could hardly believe what she was hearing. "No, you didn't trust me, Marco, and you didn't trust me because you knew that I couldn't trust you. And you knew that because you're a liar, and liars don't trust people because they know that they themselves cannot be trusted." She not only felt sick, she also felt as though she could hardly breathe. "You are Prince Marco of Niroli…. How could you not tell me who you are and still live with me as intimately as we have lived together?" she demanded brokenly.

"Stop being so ridiculously dramatic," Marco demanded fiercely. "You are making too much of the situation."

"Too much?" Emily almost screamed the words at

him. "When were you going to tell me, Marco? Perhaps you just planned to walk away without telling me anything? After all, what do my feelings matter to you?"

"Of course they matter." Marco stopped her sharply. "And it was in part to protect them, and you, that I decided not to inform you when my grandfather first announced that he intended to step down from the throne and hand it on to me."

"To protect me?" Emily nearly choked on her fury. "Hand on the throne? No wonder you told me when you first took me to bed that all you wanted was sex. You *knew* that was the only kind of relationship there could ever be between us! You *knew* that one day you would be Niroli's king. No doubt you are expected to marry a princess. Is she picked out for you already, your *royal* bride?"

* * * * *

Look for
THE FUTURE KING'S PREGNANT MISTRESS
by Penny Jordan in July 2007,
from Harlequin Presents,
available wherever books are sold.

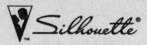

Silhouette®

Romantic
SUSPENSE

**Sparked by Danger,
Fueled by Passion.**

Mission: Impassioned

A brand-new miniseries begins with

My Spy

By *USA TODAY* bestselling author

Marie Ferrarella

She had to trust him with her life....
It was the most daring mission of Joshua Lazlo's
career: rescuing the prime minister of England's
daughter from a gang of cold-blooded kidnappers.
But nothing prepared the shadowy secret agent
for a fiery woman whose touch ignited something
far more dangerous.

My Spy

#1472

Available July 2007 wherever you buy books!

Visit Silhouette Books at www.eHarlequin.com   SRS27542

nocturne™

**DON'T MISS THE RIVETING CONCLUSION
TO THE RAINTREE TRILOGY**

RAINTREE: SANCTUARY

by *New York Times* bestselling author

BEVERLY
BARTON

Mercy, guardian of the Raintree
homeplace, takes a stand against
the Ansara wizards to battle for
the Clan's future.

*On sale July,
wherever books are sold.*

SNRT2

REQUEST YOUR FREE BOOKS!

2 FREE NOVELS PLUS 2 FREE GIFTS!

HARLEQUIN® Blaze®

Red-hot reads!

YES! Please send me 2 FREE Harlequin® Blaze® novels and my 2 FREE gifts. After receiving them, if I don't wish to receive any more books, I can return the shipping statement marked "cancel." If I don't cancel, I will receive 6 brand-new novels every month and be billed just $3.99 per book in the U.S., or $4.47 per book in Canada, plus 25¢ shipping and handling per book and applicable taxes, if any*. That's a savings of at least 15% off the cover price! I understand that accepting the 2 free books and gifts places me under no obligation to buy anything. I can always return a shipment and cancel at any time. Even if I never buy another book from Harlequin, the two free books and gifts are mine to keep forever.

151 HDN EF3W   351 HDN EF3X

Name	(PLEASE PRINT)
Address	Apt.
City	State/Prov.	Zip/Postal Code

Signature (if under 18, a parent or guardian must sign)

Mail to the **Harlequin Reader Service®**:

IN U.S.A.: P.O. Box 1867, Buffalo, NY 14240-1867
IN CANADA: P.O. Box 609, Fort Erie, Ontario L2A 5X3

Not valid to current Harlequin Blaze subscribers.

Want to try two free books from another line?
Call 1-800-873-8635 or visit www.morefreebooks.com.

* Terms and prices subject to change without notice. NY residents add applicable sales tax. Canadian residents will be charged applicable provincial taxes and GST. This offer is limited to one order per household. All orders subject to approval. Credit or debit balances in a customer's account(s) may be offset by any other outstanding balance owed by or to the customer. Please allow 4 to 6 weeks for delivery.

Your Privacy: Harlequin is committed to protecting your privacy. Our Privacy Policy is available online at www.eHarlequin.com or upon request from the Reader Service. From time to time we make our lists of customers available to reputable firms who may have a product or service of interest to you. If you would prefer we not share your name and address, please check here. ☐

HB07

THE GARRISONS

A brand-new family saga begins with

THE CEO'S SCANDALOUS AFFAIR

BY ROXANNE ST. CLAIRE

Eldest son Parker Garrison is preoccupied running
his Miami hotel empire and dealing with his recently
deceased father's secret second family. Since he has
little time to date, taking his superefficient assistant
to a charity event should have been a simple plan.
Until passion takes them beyond business.

Don't miss any of the six exciting titles in
THE GARRISONS continuity, beginning in July.
Only from Silhouette Desire.

THE CEO'S SCANDALOUS AFFAIR

#1807

Available July 2007.

Visit Silhouette Books at www.eHarlequin.com   SD76807

HARLEQUIN®
Blaze™

COMING NEXT MONTH